THE CITIZEN READER
AUSTRALIAN EDITION

This edition published 2026
by Living Book Press
Copyright © Living Book Press, 2026

ISBN: 978-1-76153-948-0 (hardcover)
         978-1-76153-927-5 (softcover)

First published in 1906.

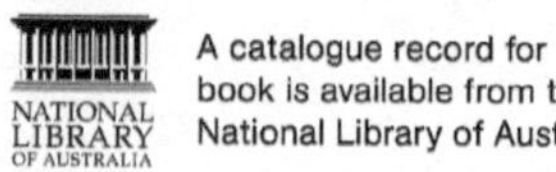

THE CITIZEN READER
AUSTRALIAN EDITION

by

H. O. ARNOLD-FORSTER

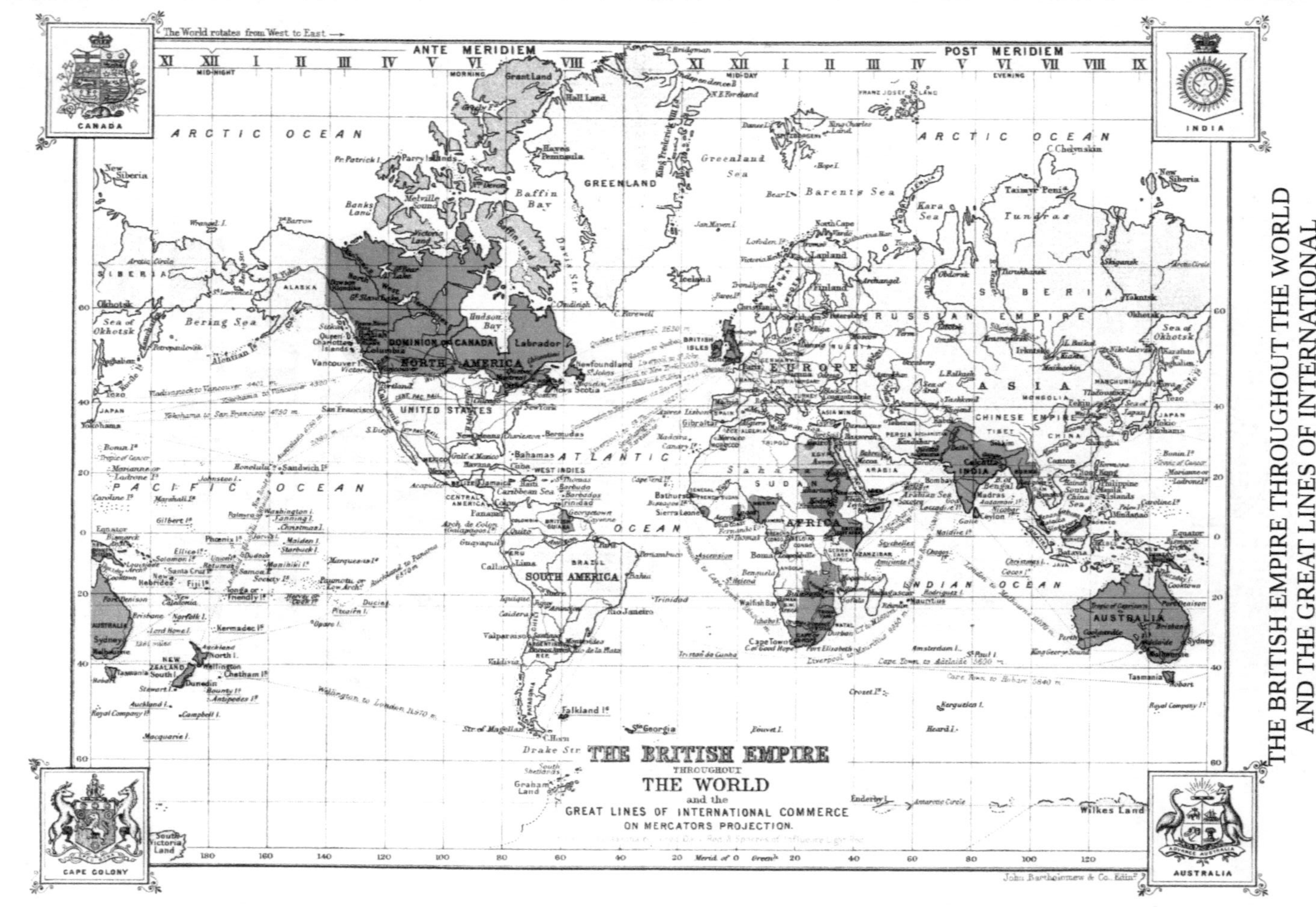

THE BRITISH EMPIRE THROUGHOUT THE WORLD
AND THE GREAT LINES OF INTERNATIONAL
COMMERCE ON MERCATORS PROJECTION.
JOHN BARTHOLOMEW & CO. EDIN.

CONTENTS

PREFACE TO THE ENGLISH EDITION 1

PREFACE TO THE AUSTRALIAN EDITION 3

INTRODUCTION 5

1. WHAT IS MEANT BY BEING A GOOD CITIZEN 7

2. PATRIOTISM. 16

3. HOW THE COUNTRY IS GOVERNED. 26

4. THE KING, HIS REPRESENTATIVES,
    AND THE PARLIAMENTS OF AUSTRALIA. 38

5. HOW THE LAWS ARE CARRIED OUT. 49

6. OUR LITTLE PARLIAMENTS 59

7. LAW AND JUSTICE. 68

8. PART 1. THE TRIAL 74

8. PART 2. THE AUTHORITY OF THE LAW. 87

9. BRITAIN'S NAVY AND ARMY. 90

10. AUSTRALIA'S DEFENCE FORCES 102

11. A SOLDIER'S TRAINING, AND WHAT IT DOES. 107

12. BRITAIN AND HER COLONIES 115

13. THE FLAG. – PART I. 120

14. THE FLAG.—PART II. 133

15. TAXATION. 141

16. OUR DUTY TOWARDS FOREIGN COUNTRIES.—PART I 152

17. OUR DUTY TOWARDS FOREIGN COUNTRIES — PART II. ... 157

18. OUR DUTY TOWARDS FOREIGN COUNTRIES — PART III ...162

19. EDUCATION. 167

20. THRIFT. 178

21. FREEDOM 185

22. HOW OUR FREEDOM WAS WON 193

23. WATCHWORDS OF ENGLISH LIBERTY. 200

PREFACE TO THE ENGLISH EDITION

THIS *Citizen Reader* seems to me a successful attempt to fill a gap in school books which I am surprised has not been filled before. There is no doubt that the enormous majority of school children will have public as well as private duties to perform—the boys, in most cases, by direct action, and the girls by indirect but powerful influence. They will be called upon not only to lead an upright life and to do what they rightly can to help those who are bound to them by family ties, but it will also be their duty to serve their country as patriotic citizens; and the fulfilment of this duty will be greatly aided by some knowledge of the institutions of their country.

The object of this book is to describe, in language which a child can understand, the principles and purpose of our institutions and the machinery of our administration, and also to tell children what ought to be the principles which should actuate them as patriotic citizens.

The last aim is without doubt a difficult one. It is not easy to fulfil it without affronting prejudices or indeed honest convictions. But I think any unbiassed reader will admit that there is little, if anything, in this book which will not be accepted by men of all creeds and parties.

It is well known that our English educational system is almost alone in the refusal of Government either to prescribe or to authorise school books. There is much to be said for and against this course, but on the other hand, the Education Code, by permitting the use of a variety of Readers in our elementary schools, gives ample opportunity for the introduction of works such as this. Already much has been done by the issue of specially prepared books to instruct children with regard to history, science, and other branches of learning. Why should not a similar effort be made to instruct them in the duties of citizenship? I need not dwell upon what must be apparent to all—namely, that there is a special fitness in the appearance of a book of this kind at a time when we have just added millions to the citizens who have the right of electing representatives.

I can therefore commend *The Citizen Reader* to the consideration of those who are interested in education, as a fair and, in my opinion, not unsuccessful attempt to supply a deficiency which has remained too long unfilled.

W. E. FORSTER

London, 1885.

PREFACE TO THE AUSTRALIAN EDITION

THOUGH educational authorities in Australia cannot be accused of neglecting the claims of history as a subject of instruction, yet it (like several other subjects, indeed) has but lately been regarded from the standpoint of practical application. The courses of English history in primary and grammar schools used to consist of outlines of the main incidents in the nation's life; and the memorising of those outlines consumed hundreds of hours of the child's time, with little result except a "pass" on the day of examination and a distaste for the reading of history.

Now, however, our programmes of instruction include Australian history, the rights and duties of citizenship (civic and moral), and a conspectus of British history.

To supply satisfactorily the urgent need of teachers and pupils under the new requirements, particularly as regards the first two topics, is a matter of much importance; and it has given me great satisfaction to have a part, through this book, in an attempt to do so.

I trust that this adaptation of *The Citizen Reader* will merit such words of commendation as those bestowed by the Right Hon. W. E. Forster on the first English edition—a book which, issued in 1885, has passed through many editions in England and in Scotland, and has been reproduced for the schools of Japan.

Though portions of the English edition were inappropriate or inadequate for use in Australia, the merits of the book prevailed over those drawbacks and caused it to be used here, to some extent, by progressive teachers; and now that it has, I trust, been rendered intelligible, from cover to cover, to the Australian child, I am hopeful that its suitability and value will be apparent to teachers generally, and that it will supply adequately the want that is felt in the schools.

On the illustrations, considerable care has been bestowed and expense incurred. It was felt that portraits of notable men, and views of public buildings, etc., in the various States, while helpful and interesting to the reader, would also aid in the promotion of a highly desirable unity of sentiment and pride of possession among the boys and girls of the new nation.

Several of the photographs in this book are from *Choice Views of Australia*, and are reproduced here by permission of the publishers of that work, the N.S.W. Bookstalls Co., and the photographers.

The many stimulating examples of heroic deeds from British history given in the original work have been retained, and also the references to great charters of British liberty; for, as Sir Henry Parkes finely said on a great occasion, "The crimson thread of kinship runs through us all."

2ND JANUARY, 1906.
C. R. L.

INTRODUCTION

THIS work is intended to instruct boys and girls in the Primary and Secondary Schools of Australia with regard to their rights, duties, and privileges as British citizens dwelling in Australia. It contains an account, in simple and popular language, of the principles of the legislative and administrative arrangements of the country, explains the meaning and value of our chief popular liberties, and describes the duties owed by British citizens to their country, their country-men, and themselves.

"The life of a people grows; it is knit together and yet expanded, in joy and sorrow, in thought and action; it absorbs the thought of other nations into its own forms, and gives back the thought as new wealth to the world; it is a power and an organ in the great body of the nations. But there may come a check, an arrest; memories may be stifled, and love may be faint for the lack of them; or memories may shrink into withered relics—the soul of a people—whereby they know themselves to be one, may seem to be dying for want of common action. But who shall say, 'The fountain of their life is dried up, they shall for ever cease to be a nation'? Who shall say it? Not he who feels the life of his people stirring within his own. Shall he say, 'That way events are wending, I will not resist'? His very soul is resistance, and is as a seed of fire that may enkindle the souls of multitudes, and make a new pathway for events."
— *GEORGE ELIOT*

"I, for one, fervently hope that our connection with the grand old State from which we sprang may long continue. I can conceive of no higher distinction for the young Australian Commonwealth than that of being affiliated to old England by some delicate but sufficiently binding ties, taking a noble, world-embracing course of progress under the same grand old flag."

— SIR HENRY PARKES

CHAPTER I.
WHAT IS MEANT BY BEING A GOOD CITIZEN

"I am a citizen of no mean city."

I. THE COUNTRY WE BELONG TO

1. THE words taken as the motto of this chapter were used by **St. Paul**, and the city of which he spoke was **Tarsus**, in Asia Minor.

2. The words he uttered may certainly be repeated by every one of us; and if St. Paul were proud of being a citizen of Tarsus, we who live in Australia, or in any part of the great British Empire, may indeed say with pride that we too are **"citizens of no mean country."**

3. Look at the map at the beginning of this book, and think what is meant by all those patches which you will see dotted over every part of it.

4. They mean that in every part of the world so marked there are countrymen of ours living and working; that in every continent and in every climate there are men and women who read the same **Bible** that we read, who enjoy the same books that we enjoy—**Shakespeare, Burns, Moore**; men and women who look back to the same history that we look back to, who speak our language, who use British law, and who are ready to share our dangers and to rejoice in our good fortune.

5. The chief authority—the source of all government—in this great Empire resides in the two little islands that make up the United Kingdom of Great Britain and Ireland, or **Britain**, as I shall fre-

quently call it. The people who now bear sway, in the name of its sovereign, over about a fourth of the land surface of the globe were either born in those islands, or their ancestors had their homes there.

Why We Are Proud of Our Country

6. I hope you are all proud of this vast British Empire to which you belong, but I trust you do not think that I wish you to be proud of it only because it is big. That would be a great mistake. It would be just as sensible to say that a man was a good man simply because he was a big one, as to say that a country was to be admired because it covered a great many square miles. You know that what makes a man great and honourable is what he does, and not what he looks like.

7. Some of the weakest and smallest men have yet been the noblest and the most useful. St. Paul himself, whose words we read just now, was a man who had no great strength; he tells us, indeed, that he was "in bodily presence weak, and in speech contemptible." It is the spirit and mind of a man that give him his power; and so it is with our own, or with any other country: it will be truly great and honourable only if it does things which in themselves are honourable and worthy. If a country does wrong, and uses its power to injure others unjustly, then, however big and strong the country may be, however victorious in war, however prosperous in peace, there will be no reason to be proud of it.

Our Country Is What We Make It

8. But I have been talking to you about the country doing right and wrong, and I think it is time you should ask me what I mean by "the Country," and how it is that I can speak about it as if I were speaking of a man or a woman?

9. When we speak of a country doing right and wrong, we mean that the people who live in it, and who decide how it shall be governed, have chosen the good way or the bad way. Who is it, then,

that makes Australia (which is more particularly *our* Country, and has been given freedom of action in very many directions by the Mother-country) do right or wrong? Who is it that makes it a country to be proud of or a country to be ashamed of? Think for yourselves a moment, and you will see that it is you, and I, and all of us who take any part in governing the Country, who decide the matter. And remember that all of you, when you grow up, will have votes, and will help to send members to Parliament, so that you will really and truly help to govern the Country.

10. But giving votes for members of Parliament is not by any means the only way in which you will be able to make a difference. If you care about doing it, you will always find plenty of ways in which you can set to work.

11. You will see now that it is no good talking about the greatness of the Country, or pretending to be proud of it, unless we who live in the Country really do something to make it great, and of which we, and those who come after us, have a right to be proud.

II. How to Become a Good Citizen

1. I am going to try in this book to explain to you what are the ways in which this Country is governed, and to show you how our laws are made, and why we should obey them; to point out the best ways in which you can serve the Country, and how you can become really good and useful citizens.

2. It is perhaps hard to understand at first how there can be any difference between being a *good citizen* and being a *good man or woman*. And in one sense, it is true, there is no difference; for a bad man or a bad woman will never be a really good citizen. But while I want you not to forget this, I want you to give your special attention to those things which people have to do for the sake of others, quite apart from their own family and friends, in order that the

Country may be wisely and justly governed, and may be respected and honoured by foreign nations.

Private Duties

3. You will easily see what I mean if I give you an example. Suppose you or I were to be living, like Robinson Crusoe, alone on an island. Although we were quite alone, we should still be just as much bound to try to do right, as far as we were able, as if we lived in a busy town.

4. We should not be cruel to animals, we should try to keep our body in health, so that our mind might be clear and healthy too; and you may be sure there are other ways also in which we should find opportunities of choosing the right or the wrong way. But if we were asked to do the duties of *a good citizen*, I certainly think we should be puzzled how to set about them.

5. And so, too, in our own families there are hundreds of ways in which we may do our duty or avoid doing it. But whether we do it or not will depend upon how we have been taught by our parents, how much we love those who are near to us, and will have very little to do with our duties as citizens.

6. But when we come to live in a great and busy country like this, where there are millions of people all working in different ways and for different ends, when we have to act in such a way that we shall do no injustice to others nor suffer injustice ourselves, then we must begin directly to think about what I will call *public duty*, and we must make up our minds how we should behave so that not only we in our own homes shall be happy and prosperous, but that all our fellow countrymen, rich and poor, high and low, may be happy and prosperous too. To learn how to do this is to learn how to become *a good citizen*.

The Common Rule

7. But though the things we may have to do as citizens are different from what we have to do as private people among our own family and friends, there is no difference in the rules which ought to guide us in the one case and in the other, and that is why it is worth while to begin thinking about these questions while we are young and still at school.

8. The very same lessons of kindness, truth, honour, and obedience which you learn at home from **your parents**, at school from **your teachers**, and in church or chapel from **your clergymen, ministers,** and **priests**, have to be remembered and acted upon when you grow up, and become **voters**, or **taxpayers, soldiers, sailors**, or **jurymen**: in fact, in all the things which you may ever have to do for the good of your country and the welfare of your countrymen.

9. Just as at home it is sometimes your duty to deny yourself some amusement or advantage for the sake of your mother, sisters, or friends; or, again, as you may possibly have to suffer some pain or inconvenience for their good; so it often becomes the duty of men and women to deny themselves a great many advantages, to suffer loss or pain—not that their own friends and relations among whom they live may be the better, but that all the people of this country may gain, that the country may do what is just and right—that the country may help, and not injure, those who live in foreign countries.

How Lancashire did its Duty.

10. I will give you one or two examples of men and women doing their duty in this way as citizens, which will show you what I mean better than I can explain it to you.

11. In the year 1861 a great war broke out in the **United States of America**. It was one of those terrible wars which are called "civil wars"; that is to say, those who fought on either side belonged to the same nation, and were really one people.

12. The war began about a dispute between the **States in the North** and the **States in the South** as to their exact rights of interfering with each other in the making of laws. But before long it became quite clear that the real question which both sides were determined to settle was a very different one—it was the question whether there should be any more slaves in the United States or not.

13. The **Northern States** had given up slavery themselves, and they were determined that it should come to an end in the South too. The **Southerners**, who employed the slaves to cultivate their cotton plantations, were equally determined not to give up their right to buy and sell the negroes, and to make them work for them for nothing. But you will perhaps ask what had all this got to do with British citizens and their duties. I am coming to that; and when I have told you a little more, I think you will see that it has a great deal to do with them.

14. I said that the "Southerners" required their slaves to cultivate the cotton for them. The cotton, as you know, is a plant from the pod of which is taken the material which is spun into calico to make shirts and handkerchiefs and a hundred other things which we use every day.

15. At the time of the war in the United States, nearly all the cotton grown in the South was sent to **Lancashire**, and there spun and woven in the mills by English factory hands. No less than 800,000 people were employed in the various mills. But before the war had been going on long, it became clear that the cotton would be prevented from reaching Liverpool, for in order to conquer the Southern States, the Northern States ordered their ships to stop all vessels carrying cotton from the Southern harbours. What is called a *blockade* was declared, and the different ports were soon really blocked.

16. This all happened thousands of miles away from Britain, but its effect was very soon felt there. In Lancashire, the supply of cotton ran short, the mills were compelled to stop running, and

SLAVES ON A COTTON PLANTATION.

the thousands of people who were employed in them were thrown out of work. To be out of work was to be out of wages, and before long many were actually starving, while very many were supported by charity only. The distress increased even faster than the means of relief, and although nearly three million pounds were given by the Government, or subscribed by friends of the sufferers, the greatest misery prevailed.

17. It was plain to everybody that if the South were to be victorious, or if the North were made to give up the blockade, the cotton would soon begin to pour into Liverpool again, and there were many people in Britain at the time who did all they could to help the South, and to try to make Parliament take their part.

18. But in spite of their suffering, the working men of Lancashire would never consent to help the cause of slavery. They knew that across the Atlantic the Northerners were fighting in the cause of **freedom** and **justice** against the bullets of the enemy. They were

determined that they at least would not make the battle harder for the friends of right, and that, at any rate as far as they were concerned, their country should do its duty, even though they had to suffer for it.

19. And so, as good citizens, they put into practice the rule of right which they had learnt to be a just one in their own families and their own business, and they stood up all through the war for the cause of liberty. Lancashire would not join in the cry against the North, and thus the British Government was able to keep up its friendship with the United States, and to avoid the terrible consequences of a great war. This is an instance of how we can do our duty as citizens in big things, but I could give you plenty of examples of how needful it is to do it in small things too.

III. How We Can Help the Country.

1. Every time one of us is **courteous and civil to a foreigner**, he is doing his part as a good citizen, for he is helping to make his country liked and respected abroad. Every time a man walks to the polling place and **gives his vote honestly** for a member of Parliament, he is doing his part as a good citizen in helping to make the government of the country honest and fair.

2. Every time a **mother** sends her child to school, she is doing her duty as a good citizen, for the law says that all children must be educated, and it is the part of a good citizen to obey the law. Moreover, **every boy or girl** who goes to school willingly and cheerfully is doing his or her duty as a good citizen, for of course it would be no good at all for the law to send children to school if the children themselves wasted their time and neglected their work when they got there.

3. So you will see that there are many ways, both great and small, in which we may all of us show that we are good citizens, and are willing to serve our country.

4. And lastly, there is one other and most important way in which

we may help our country, help our neighbours, and help ourselves, and that is to be careful in our own lives to live honestly and well; for no amount of good laws, no amount of famous victories, and no riches will make a country great if the people who live in it do not try themselves to be *true and just in all their dealings*—remembering that to rule oneself is the first step to being able to rule others.

Two Ways of Doing Our Duty.

5. These and all the other things which I shall have to mention to you are matters with which every one of you may at some time or another have to do when you grow up. Some of them, indeed, you have a good deal to do with now.

6. There will always be two ways of doing your duty as good citizens. The one way is to do it because you are obliged, and because you cannot help it. The other, and the better way, is to do it because you understand it, and because you feel that in doing it well you are helping at the same time your Country, your countrymen, and yourself. We very often have to do things during our lives of which we do not understand the reasons, but the more clearly we understand the work we have to do—depend upon it—the better the work will be done.

7. And now I must come to the real lessons I want you to learn in order that you may become good and useful citizens. There are some rules we must all learn, and some things we must all be able to do; but the most important thing of all is to learn what we have to learn and to do what we have to do in the proper spirit.

8. And that is why, before I tell you anything about laws and law-making, and voting, and other very important matters, I am going to give up a chapter to explaining to you what is meant by *Patriotism*, because if you understand that, you will see also how in all that we do as citizens we can serve our Country as well as ourselves.

CHAPTER II.
PATRIOTISM.

"Not once nor twice in our rough island story
The path of duty was the way to glory." — *Tennyson.*

"One people, one destiny." — *Sir Henry Parkes.*

IV. WHAT THE WORD MEANS.

1. PATRIOTISM comes from the Latin word *Patria*[1], and means love of one's country or of one's Fatherland. The words *patriotism* and *patriotic* are often misused and misunderstood, but, when properly and truly understood, they describe a great and worthy feeling which ought to fill the mind of every man and woman. It is right that all men and women should love the country in which they live, and on whose good fortune their own happiness depends. You all know that the first love which we have is for our own family and our own friends: we wish them to succeed, and we wish them to be happy; nay, more, we try to make them so.

2. And what is true of the small circle of our friends and relations is true also of the larger circles into which we are brought as we grow older. Boys and girls, when they go to school, are nearly always proud of their school, and are anxious for its credit and good name. A boy wishes his own school to be the best at cricket, at football, at examinations, in winning scholarships, in work, and in play; and you will see just the same thing among grown-up people. Each nation

---

1   *Pater* means father; *Patria*, fatherland.

of the British Empire—Australia, New Zealand, Canada, South Africa—each state or district that goes to form them, and even each township in them, will be proud of its own history and anxious to add to its own good fame.

3. If it be rightly understood and rightly acted upon, this feeling is a very good and a very helpful one, for a man who tries to do better than his neighbour must needs do well himself. A schoolboy who tries to keep up the credit of his school, a rifleman who longs to add to the fame of his corps, will always feel that much is expected of him by others, and, as a rule, a boy or a man will do more the more you expect of him.

4. And so it is with **patriotism** and the **love of country**: those who really love their country will be particularly careful not to do anything by which it may be dishonoured. On the other hand, they will always try with all their power to place their country before all others in every right and noble work; and so it comes about that they will often give up their lives and their fortunes, not that their own immediate friends and families may be the gainers, but in order that their country may be saved from danger, and that others may think well of it.

5. There are many instances in the long history of the British Empire in which countrymen of ours have given up life and wealth for their country, and we who are alive now owe much to what they have suffered and sacrificed.

THE TRUE PATRIOT.

6. Every British citizen ought to remember one very important thing about the patriotism which has made the British Empire what it is. Those who love their country best are content to serve it without the hope of immediate reward, or even the encouragement of praise.

7. Sometimes it may be that the very act which is performed for the sake of one's country is done far away from any friendly eye,

with no certainty that friends at home will ever even know of it, and yet, for the sake of duty and love of country, the deed will be done.

The Magazine at Delhi.

8. There is a story of a brave action, done during the great mutiny in India, which will show you very clearly what I mean. It was at the time when the **Sepoys**, or native soldiers, in a great part of India had risen against their British rulers. In many places all the white people

WILLOUGHBY'S BRAVE DEED.

had been killed; in others they had been shut up and besieged in different forts and towns. There were very few British soldiers ready, and it seemed at one time as if every English-speaking man, woman, and child would be killed or driven out of India.

9. The great city of **Delhi**, in the north of India, was surrounded by Sepoys, and had they taken it, the danger would at once have increased tenfold, for at Delhi was the great magazine in which were kept the gunpowder, the arms, and the stores which the British Government had provided for the use of the army. If once the Sepoys had got possession of the powder and arms, they would doubtless have been able to beat our small armies and to gain a complete victory.

10. But into the magazine at Delhi the Sepoys never got, for in it were a handful of British soldiers who were determined that, if the sacrifice of their lives could prevent it, the danger of their fellow-countrymen should not be increased. The enemy surrounded the magazine. Lieutenant Willoughby and his brave comrades knew well that to defend it was impossible, but they were determined that it should not be taken.

11. A train of gunpowder was laid down to the magazine, and as the enemy began to swarm over the walls, Willoughby gave the signal to light the match. "A roar followed as if the earth were splitting asunder, and while all Delhi, from the bank of the Jumna to the Cashmere Gate, shook and trembled, the mighty magazine exploded, and for a time a dark cloud overhung the palace and the city. Hundreds of the mutineers were blown into the air, but none of the brave defenders escaped without injury."

12. Conductor Scully was so dreadfully wounded that for him escape was impossible. Willoughby and Forrest succeeded in reaching the Cashmere Gate. The latter escaped, and the former was murdered on the road to Meerut; but Buckley and another reached headquarters in safety.

13. Such is the story of the **Magazine of Delhi**. What I want

you to notice in it is that these men who thus risked their lives for their country did so far away from the eye of friends, and without any of the encouragement which cheers those who do their duty in the sight of friends and with the hope of reward.

V. THE STORY OF COLUMBUS, AND ITS LESSON.

1. Sometimes men and women may act in what they believe the best way for their country, even though, at the time, the wisdom and usefulness of what they are doing is not seen by those among whom they live, and their only reward, at the time, is hatred and mistrust. Not till long after is the good work they have done seen and understood by their countrymen.

2. Some of you will perhaps remember the story of Columbus, the great discoverer of America. What a difference to the world Columbus's discovery has made it is impossible to exaggerate. Yet, at the time, neither was the importance of his work understood by his countrymen, nor did he himself receive the honour and encouragement which his bravery and his perseverance deserved. The story of Columbus and his adventures is a very sad one.

3. Four times did Columbus cross the Atlantic Ocean in the service of his country. The wonders of the New World were, for the first time, thrown open to those who lived in the Old World by his courage, his perseverance, and his skill. And what was the reward which he received during his lifetime for what he had done? Abandoned in his old age by Ferdinand of Spain, to whose power and wealth he had added so much, he was refused not only generous treatment, but even a fair hearing for his claims.

4. Suffering from a painful illness, and worn out with the hardships of a life of danger and exposure, he tried in vain to gain favour of the Court, if not for himself, at least for his son, whom he was leaving behind him. The King was deaf to his appeal, and the greatest discoverer the world has ever known was left to die in sorrow and pain.

5. Let me give you an account of the death of Columbus by the great American writer, Washington Irving:—

"The cares and troubles of Columbus were drawing to a close. The momentary fire which had reanimated him was soon quenched by accumulating infirmities. His last voyage shattered beyond repair a frame already worn and wasted by a life of hardships; and continual anxieties robbed him of that repose so necessary to remit the weariness and debility of age.

6. "The cold ingratitude of his sovereign chilled his heart. The continual suspension of his honours, and the enmity and defamation experienced at every turn, seemed to throw a shadow over that glory which had been the great object of his ambition. This shadow, it is true, could be but of transient duration; but it is difficult for the most illustrious man to look beyond the present cloud which may obscure his fame, and anticipate its permanent lustre in the admiration of posterity."

7. We, who have seen the cloud lifted, and who know that, in our day, Columbus's great work is fully understood, and that he himself is remembered not only by his own country Spain, but by all countries both in Europe and America, as one of the noblest of the world's heroes, can feel true sorrow for the poor dying man, to whom the injustice of his lot was so clear, and who could not know what honour would be paid to his name when he was dead.

8. More than this, we may find in his story an example of how the greatest services may be rendered to a nation or to the world by a man who, while he is doing his work, receives neither honour nor reward from his countrymen.

9. And in the history of the British Empire there always have been, and always will be, men who, like Columbus, have done some great work or found out some great truth which they have longed to put at the disposal of their countrymen. But the truth has been rejected,

COLUMBUS APPEARING BEFORE THE
KING AND QUEEN OF SPAIN

the service declined, and the man himself has had only suffering and disappointment for his efforts.

10. Not until his life was over did the seed which he had sown bear fruit, or the discovery he had made fall into other hands better able to use it. But, in the long run, the country has got the benefit of his work, and has learned to recognise a true patriot in the man who was despised and persecuted during his lifetime.

VI. FALSE PATRIOTISM.

1. There is, however, **a false and a bad side to patriotism**, which it is well to remember. You will sometimes hear people talk as if it were always right to support what is done by our own people in foreign countries, whether what they have done be right or wrong, only because those who have done it are British. This is wrong in itself, and can only lead us into troubles and difficulties; for it is plain that if we think it right to approve of or to overlook bad actions because our countrymen do them, it is equally likely that a Frenchman or a German will do the same when his countrymen make mistakes or commit faults.

2. And so, all the world over, we should have great nations like Britain, Germany, and France supporting what they knew to be wrong for the sake of a false patriotism.

Be Just, and Fear Not.

3. Then, again, I need not tell you that it is not always those who are most ready to go to war who are really the most patriotic. Sometimes, indeed, when all one's friends and neighbours are in favour of war, it requires more true bravery and true patriotism to speak up for peace than would be required even to go and fight in the war.

4. In the time of George III., the King and the Parliament wished to govern the English who had gone to America, and to govern them in a way which was contrary to their wishes and without their advice.

5. When the **Colonists**—for so the British in America were then called—refused to obey a Parliament which they had not chosen, King George and the Parliament declared war upon them, and sent soldiers to put them down. But there were some men in Britain who could not believe that it was right or just to make Britons obey laws which they themselves had had no share in making, and, despite the King and the majority of Parliament being against them, they had the courage to say so openly, and to try to obtain for their countrymen across the Atlantic the same rights which they claimed for themselves.

6. The greatest of these men was **Edmund Burke**, whose famous writings I hope you will read some day. Although many of his friends were anxious for war, and though by refusing to support the King he lost favour at Court, he nevertheless raised his voice over and over again on behalf of peace.

7. Unfortunately, he was not listened to; unluckily, those who cried out for war were listened to. The war went on; the colonists rose against the Royal troops and defeated them, and at last, as we know, the colonists refused any longer to submit to British rule, and made a government and a nation of their own. The nation became the **"United States of America."**

8. It is impossible to say what would have been the future of Britain and the United States if the wise counsel of Edmund Burke had been followed. But of one thing we may be sure, namely, that all the suffering and sorrow caused by an unjust war would have been avoided, and that the hatred and distrust, which for a long time after the war existed between the British at home and their brethren in America, would not have been felt.

9. Happily, the bitter memories of that time are long forgotten, and today between Britain and the United States there are only feelings of friendship and brotherhood; but we can all see now how much better it would have been if Burke's words in favour of peace had prevailed; and we can see in him **a true patriot**, because he was brave

EDMUND BURKE
FROM THE PORTRAIT BY SIR
JOSHUA REYNOLDS.
*(PHOTO: WALKER & COCKERELL,
CLIFFORD'S IN, E.C.)*

enough to say before all the world that he would not support what he thought to be unjust and wrong.

10. Thus you will see that there are many ways in which patriotism can be shown. And you will understand how necessary it is to distinguish true patriotism from that which is false.

11. Now that I have explained to you what is meant by being a good citizen, I shall give you some account of the different duties which a good citizen has to perform, of the laws by which he is governed, of the advantages which he enjoys. I shall tell you how the laws are made, and who it is makes them. I shall show you how the Country is defended from its enemies abroad, and how good order and contentment are secured at home.

12. I want you also to learn something about the arrangements which are made for carrying out the law, for trying and punishing those who break it, and for protecting those who obey it.

CHAPTER III.
HOW THE COUNTRY IS GOVERNED.

"Now call we our high court of Parliament,
And let us choose such limbs of noble council,
That the great body of our state may go
In equal rank with the best govern'd nation."
Henry IV., Pt. II., Act V., Sc. 2.

No vassal progeny of subject brood,
No satellite shed from Britain's plenitude,
But orbed with her in one wide sphere of good."
Brunton Stephens.

VII. WHO GOVERNS.

1. I TOLD you that, before any one of us could be a useful citizen, it was necessary that we should know something **of the laws of the Country** in which we live, should understand some of the chief reasons for those laws, and be acquainted with the ways in which they are made and carried out.

2. All of you, when you reach manhood or womanhood, will have to do with governing the Country, and will have to obey the laws by which it is governed, so it is really necessary for you to learn, as soon as possible, something about these important matters.

3. How is the Country governed? **"By the Government,"** is the first answer that you will be likely to give, and in a way the answer is right. But **who governs the Government?** The answer is that **Parliament** does. But last of all, **who governs Parliament?** And

the answer to that is that the **People of this Country** govern Parliament. And so you will see that the real answer to the question, "Who governs the Country?" is, "**The Country governs itself.**"

4. This was not always so in England. At one time **the King** alone governed the Country; at another time it was **the King together with a few powerful lords**; and till well on in the nineteenth century, although Parliament was supposed to decide all matters of government, Parliament itself was only elected by a few people, and so the Country did not really govern itself. It was only in 1884 that **the vote** was given to almost every man of full age.

5. Nor was it always so in Australia: we have reached, through several stages, our system of governing ourselves. Let me glance briefly at them.

6. It was in 1788 that the first settlement by white people was made on our island continent—afterwards to receive the name of Australia—and that settlement was British. On the shores of Port Jackson, a governor, with a few officials and a regiment of soldiers, ruled in the name of the King of Great Britain over the colonists, most of whom were men and women who had committed some crime—perhaps not a very serious one—but deemed sufficient, in those days, to justify the sentence of transportation to a land far distant from home.

7. These convicts were, of course, not allowed to have a voice in making laws for the settlement; nor, indeed, for many years, were the free settlers. The latter, as time went on, became numerous, not only around Sydney, but in other parts, and succeeded in putting an end to the transportation system as far as the eastern portion of Australia was concerned.

8. After the discovery of gold in New South Wales and Victoria in 1851, the population increased very much in parts of Australia, and the British Parliament sanctioned the formation of several Parliaments, and gave them power to make laws for each portion

THE CIRCULAR QUAY, SYDNEY

called a colony, to impose taxes within its borders, and to spend the money obtained. Sydney, Melbourne, Adelaide, Hobart, Brisbane, and (though much later than the others) Perth, each became the seat of a Parliament.

9. In 1900, further authority was granted by the British Parliament to form a federal governing body for all Australia and Tasmania (to be known as the Parliament of the Commonwealth of Australia), so that laws might be made on matters, such as defence and commerce, that affect the people as a whole.

10. You have noticed the sentences, "The British Parliament sanctioned," "Further authority was granted by the British Parliament," which indicate that the supreme power resides in that body, though, in the cases mentioned, it took no action till requested to do so by the people concerned.

11. The **British** (or, as it is often called, the **Imperial**) **Parliament** consists of the **Sovereign** of the United Kingdom of Great Britain and Ireland, the **House of Lords** (the members of which are noblemen and bishops, whose rank or position gives them their seats), and the **House of Commons**, whose members are elected by the men of full age (over twenty-one years) of the kingdom.

12. I have used the words "Parliament," "members," and "elected" several times; and it will be well, before proceeding further, to make their meaning clear.

Parliament.

13. I told you that the **Country governed itself**, but, of course, it would be quite absurd to think that every man, whatever his position, and whatever his work, could really find time, or be able to give orders and to arrange matters for the public good.

14. There is only one way in which all the millions of busy people who have their living to get, and who yet wish to take some part in governing the Country, can make their wishes known. Instead of

THE LATE SIR HENRY PARKES.

going themselves to Parliament, they choose a man in whom they can trust to go there for them, and to look after their interests when he gets there.

15. As you know, the man who is sent is called the **Member**, and those who send him are called his **Constituents** or **Electors**. Members are elected to go either to the Federal Parliament to make laws for the Commonwealth, or to one of the State Parliaments to do similar work for the State on matters that concern it only.

16. I shall tell you later what is the work that has to be done by these Parliaments in governing the Country; but first, you will learn a little about the **members of the Federal Parliament**, and about the way in which they are elected. If you do this carefully, it will not be necessary to trouble much about the election of members of the **State Parliaments**, as the differences between the two methods of carrying out the work are not great.

VIII. VOTING.

1. All persons over twenty-one years of age and not criminal or insane, who have lived in Australia or Tasmania for six months, and are British subjects by birth or naturalisation, have the **right to vote** for a member of the Parliament of the Commonwealth. **Every girl and boy may, therefore, look forward to becoming an elector one day.**

2. Before the election time arrives, those who hope to be members of Parliament speak at meetings in various parts of the electorate they wish to represent, and tell the electors what are their views, and what they intend to do when they get into Parliament. Then, when the day for giving the votes comes, the **polling** or **voting** begins. Each voter goes into the voting office, and, without anyone seeing him, marks on a piece of paper a cross—so, X—opposite the name of the person whom he wishes to send to Parliament. This paper is called the "**ballot-paper**," and when he has marked it, he puts it into a big

THE OPENING OF THE FIRST PARLIAMENT OF THE
COMMONWEALTH OF AUSTRALIA, 9TH MAY, 1901

box with a hole in the top, which is called the "**ballot-box**." Here is a picture of the ballot-paper. You will see that the voter in this case

BROWN, JOHN EDWARD..	
SMITH, WALTER JAMES..	X

has given his vote to Smith, by marking his X opposite the name **SMITH, WALTER JAMES**, on the paper.[2]

3. At the end of the day, the ballot-boxes are shut up and taken away to one place, where all the papers are opened and placed in separate heaps, according to the names marked upon them. When they are all counted, the one who has the majority or largest number of votes is declared elected, and becomes the member of Parliament for the place in which the election has been held.

4. Thus, if, on counting, the numbers are found to be—

Smitt .... 10,742 votes
Brown .... 9,830 votes

then, if there be only one member to be elected, Smith will be the one chosen. This is all that is done on the polling day—at least, it is all that you would see happen if you were to be at the polling booth on the day of the election.

The Duty of Voters.

5. But a great deal more has been done really, or, at any rate, ought to have been done. For every single vote that has been given may make a difference to the Country, and may go to help or to harm it, according as it is given in favour of a wise and honest member, or

2   Another method is for the voter to strike out the name of the candidate (or candidates) whom he does not favour.

PARLIAMENT HOUSE, SPRING STREET, MELBOURNE.

in favour of one who goes to Parliament in a bad cause or without due care for the trust which has been given to him.

6. And here I should like you to think for a moment how important it is that votes should be given carefully, and how seriously every voter ought to consider what he is doing when he folds up his paper and drops it into the ballot-box. For by dropping his vote into the box, he is helping to elect a member of the Federal Parliament—a body of men which can do much good or much harm to his native land.

7. And so, when you come to be voters, be sure to consider carefully what you do with your vote. Try to make sure that the man to whom you give it has some knowledge of the work he has to do; for governing a country is no easy matter, and requires special knowledge, just as making shoes or weaving cloth does.

8. Make sure, too, that he is going to Parliament with the intention of doing all he can for the Country, and not for himself or for his own friends. Sometimes men go into Parliament to make a name for themselves, or to get advancement in life. But, after all, they can only get into Parliament because the electors have chosen them, so it becomes the business of the electors to try to find out before they vote what their member really intends to do.

IX. THE BALLOT.

1. You know I told you that, when a voter went to the polling place, he marked his cross on the paper *secretly*, and no one could know by whom each separate paper was put into the box.

This is done in order that each voter may vote according to his own true opinion and belief, and without fear or the hope of reward.

Bribery.

2. At one time, it was not uncommon in England for those who wished to become members of Parliament to pay money to the voters—to **bribe** them—to vote in their favour. Sometimes, also, they

used to threaten to do some harm to the voters if they did not support them; for instance, they would threaten to turn them out of their houses, to dismiss them from their employment, or to injure their custom if they were shopkeepers, and by these and other means try to drive the electors into voting for them—not because they wished to do so, but because they were afraid to refuse.

3. I am sorry to say that, even now, these things are done sometimes; but you will understand that, under the ballot, when every man votes in secret, it is not very much use either to bribe or to threaten, for, after all, nobody knows, when the voting is over, who it is that has given each particular vote.

4. Thus, if a mill-owner who is seeking to be a member of Parliament were to say nowadays to his workmen, "If you do not vote for me, I will punish you by turning you out of work"; or if he were to go farther and say, "If you will vote for me, I will give you a sum of money," he could never be certain, after all, whether those whom he threatened or those whom he bribed had really voted for or against

VOTING BY BALLOT.

him. So **the ballot is really a great protection**, and helps people to vote without fear, exactly as they wish.

5. Of course, if everybody were quite honest—if those who wanted to become members of Parliament were always ashamed to bribe or to threaten the voters, and the voters, on the other hand, were always too honest to receive bribes and too courageous to be afraid of threats—then there would be no need for the ballot, and everybody might vote openly and declare his opinions before all the world, which, indeed, would be much the best way. But, unfortunately, we cannot be sure that everybody will be both honest and courageous, so for the present, at any rate, we must keep to the plan of voting in secret.

6. The law says that it is very wrong to give or to receive bribes, and those who are discovered to have done either the one or the other are severely punished. This is not only law, but it is good sense; for **to buy and sell votes is to buy and sell the happiness and prosperity of the country**—to do an injury not only to ourselves, but to all our countrymen, who are certain to suffer if people are sent to Parliament, not because they are wise and fit, but because they are rich and ready to use their riches in a bad way.

7. Now I have given you some account of how members of the **Federal Parliament** are elected. It is the King's representative (the Governor-General) and this Parliament who together make the laws by which we are all governed; and law-making is such an important thing that I had better commence a fresh chapter in order to tell you about it. Before I do so, I must remind you that all our laws are not made by the Federal Parliament. Many have been, and many will be, made by each of the State Parliaments; but these laws apply merely to the people within the State boundaries.

CHAPTER IV.
THE KING, HIS REPRESENTATIVES, AND THE PARLIAMENTS OF AUSTRALIA.

"For the first time in the world's history, there will be a nation for a continent, and a continent for a nation."
— *Sir Edmund Barton.*

"Daughter am I in my mother's house, mistress in mine own."
— *Kipling.*

X. HOW ACTS OF PARLIAMENT ARE MADE.

1. **All government in our country is carried on according to law.** Taxes are paid according to law; schools are built according to law; judges are appointed and criminals are punished according to law; in short, in all we do, we are bound to act either according to law, or, at any rate, not contrary to it.

2. How, then, is this law, which makes so much difference to all of us, fixed? It is fixed by **Act of Parliament**, and an Act of Parliament has to be passed either by the Federal Parliament for the whole of Australia, or by a State Parliament for its particular State, and agreed to by the King's representative—the Governor-General in the former case, a State Governor in the latter.

The King, the Governor-General, the State Governors.

3. *The King.* — His Majesty is at the head of the Government not merely of the British Islands, but of the whole British Empire. **King George V.** is not, like King Edward I. or Queen Elizabeth,

sovereign simply by the right of being the son or daughter of a king. He does not claim to rule over this Empire by right, but he is King because he is descended from King George III., who, in his turn, was descended from George I., who was made King of Great Britain and Ireland by Parliament; that is to say, by the people of those Islands.

4. King George V., therefore, reigns by the highest title that any king or queen can ever claim to reign by. He reigns by the will of the people. As long as the great majority of British people wish that he and his descendants should reign over them, so long will he and they be powerful and respected. Our King, unlike some of his ancestors, acts in all things in accordance with the laws of the land, and in the interests of all his subjects alike.

5. The British people who live under his rule believe that they can be best governed by a king or queen, and when we look at the steady and good government of this country, we see that they are right in their belief.

6. So long, therefore, as the King reigns by the will of his subjects, we are bound to honour and to obey him. **King George** we may honour for his own sake, for he has always shown that he loves the nation over which he reigns; and besides loving him for his own sake, we should honour and obey him because he is accepted by the many millions of our countrymen as the **head of the Government**.

7. *The Governor-General.* — As I have said, the **King is represented** in the Commonwealth by the Governor-General. This officer, who is appointed by the Crown (that is, His Majesty acting with the advice of his Ministers) for a term of five or six years, receives a salary of £10,000 per annum out of the Commonwealth funds.

8. *State Governors.* — There is also a Governor associated with each State Parliament to **act for the King**.

9. Thus, we have living in our midst seven gentlemen who serve as links between us and the Imperial Government, and occupy the position of social leaders in the community. In political matters, they

usually **follow the advice of their Ministers**, but it is sometimes the duty of a Governor to set aside that advice in reference to dissolving Parliament, and decide for himself whether there shall be a new election of members or not.

The Parliaments of Australia

A. — THE FEDERAL PARLIAMENT.

10. The power of the Commonwealth of Australia to make laws is vested in a Federal Parliament, which consists of the **King** of the United Kingdom, the **Senate**, and the **House of Representatives**. Provision is made for the meeting of Parliament once at least every year.

11. *The King*. — You have seen that he is represented by the Governor-General, whose chief duties I have already mentioned.

12. *The Senate*. — This body consists of six representatives from each of the States of the Commonwealth, and has a continued existence.[3] The members are chosen for a period of six years by the people, each State, excepting Queensland, being regarded as one electorate.

13. *The House Of Representatives*. — There are about twice as many members of the House of Representatives as there are members of the Senate; and each State sends a number proportional to its population. Thus, the representation in the Senate is a representation of the *States* of the Commonwealth; that in the House of Representatives, of the *people*. Though New South Wales — the State with the greatest population — would be the strongest in the House of Representatives if all its representatives decided to vote the same way on any question, yet, in the Senate, it would have no greater voting

3   To secure this, half the Senators first elected had to retire at the end of three years. There is, however, provision for dissolving the Senate in the case of a "deadlock" — prolonged conflict of opinion — between it and the House of Representatives.

KING GEORGE V. READING THE
DECLARATION AT HIS CORONATION.

power than Tasmania — the State with the least population. Such an arrangement, it is clear, was necessary before the States with a small population would consent to come into the Federation.

14. A State is divided into areas called "**electoral divisions**" or electorates, each containing about the same number of electors, who return one member. This member receives as **remuneration** £600 a year, as also does a Senator.

15. The House of Representatives **cannot sit longer than three years**, and it may be dissolved, or brought to an end sooner, by the Governor-General.

B. — THE STATE PARLIAMENTS.

16. The State Parliaments were in existence, as you already know, before the Commonwealth Parliament, and remain as **free** to-day as they ever were **to make laws on matters not surrendered to** that body. When the six Colonies agreed to form a Federation for national purposes, they decided not to give up the rights and privileges they possessed in local affairs.

17. Each State Parliament, like that of the Commonwealth, consists of two Houses — an **Upper** and a **Lower** — a **Legislative Council** and a **Legislative Assembly** (or House of Assembly, as it is called in South Australia, Tasmania, and W. Australia). In this Parliament, conjoined with the King, the legislative power of each State resides.

18. *The King.* — A Governor, as you know, represents His Majesty.

19. *The Legislative Council.* — This body corresponds, in a measure, to the House of Lords. The framers of the Constitution under which the various Parliaments were formed sought to give the **Council more stability** than the Assembly, so that it might **act as a check** upon hasty legislation in that chamber. In New South Wales and Queensland, the members are **nominated** for life by the

LORD HOPETOUN (LATER MARQUIS OF LINLITHGOW).
(FIRST GOVERNOR-GENERAL OF THE
COMMONWEALTH OF AUSTRALIA.)

Governor, with the advice of the Ministry. In the other States, the members are **elected** for six years; they receive no allowance (except in South Australia, Western Australia, and Tasmania); the electorates are large; and the electors must possess a property or an educational qualification. Furthermore, the Council is a continuous body; it does not dissolve.[4]

20. *The Legislative Assembly*. — The Assembly is the **more popular chamber**, having about **twice as many** members as the Council, and these elected upon the basis of **adult suffrage**.[5] In every State, its duration is limited to **three years**, unless it is dissolved by the Governor. Its members receive an annual salary.

The Conduct of Business in Parliament

21. Let me tell you now a little about the method of conducting business in the Federal Parliament.

22. The members from all parts of Australia assemble at the capital, where there is a building called **Parliament House**. It contains two large rooms — one for the **Senators**, and the other for the **Representatives**, to meet in. From among themselves, the Senators choose a President, and the Representatives a Speaker, to keep order and settle any disputes that may arise. In the conduct of business, the rules and usages of the British House of Commons — the mother of Parliaments — are followed.

23. Both the Senate and the House of Representatives are arranged in such a way that the members sit facing each other on either side. The party that sits on one side is called the **Government Party**, that which sits on the other is called the **Opposition**. In the picture, you will see how the House of Representatives is arranged. The seats on the left of the picture are called the **Government benches**, those on the right the Opposition benches. In the big chair at the end sits the **Speaker**, who thus has the Government and its supporters on his right, and the Opposition on his left.

24. Now that we have some notion of the functions of the Gov-

4   In South Australia, in certain circumstances, it may be dissolved.
5   Women of full age (over twenty-one years), as well as men, have the right to vote.

THE LEGISLATIVE ASSEMBLY OF VICTORIA IN SESSION.

ernor-General, the Senate, and the House of Representatives, we can go on and see what it is that each of them does, and how it is they make laws between them.

XI. HOW LAWS ARE MADE BY THE FEDERAL PARLIAMENT.

1. Before a law can be made, someone, either in the Senate or the House of Representatives, must bring in what is called a *Bill*; that is to say, a printed statement of the new law he wishes to make, or of the alteration in the old law which he desires. Bills which, if they are passed, will compel people to pay taxes can only be brought forward in the House of Representatives, and the Senate cannot alter them.

2. When a **Bill** has been brought in, it is debated, or talked over by both parties, and is altered first in one way and then in another. If the members cannot agree about any point, then the House *divides*; that is to say, all who think one way go to one side of the chamber, and those who think the other way go to the other. They are then counted, and **the majority**, that is to say, the greater number, get their way.

An Act of Parliament.

3. When all the alterations that anyone wants to make are settled, the Bill itself is *read*, and voted upon. Before it is allowed to pass altogether, a Bill has to be read **and passed by a majority three times,** both in the Senate and in the House of Representatives. For a Bill that is brought in in the Senate has to pass through the Representatives afterwards, and one that is brought in in the Representatives has to go afterwards through the Senate.

The Royal Assent.

4. When both Houses have passed the Bill, it goes, for the King's assent, before the Governor-General, and he has to **assent** to it **or** to **refuse** it, or he may, in certain circumstances, reserve it for the King's

pleasure. Really, when a Bill has passed through both Houses of Parliament, the Governor-General always gives his assent (unless the Bill is of such a nature[6] that it must be reserved), for you must remember that he follows the advice of his Ministers in Parliament; so what his Ministers have approved, the Governor-General approves too.

The Law of the Land.

5. When the Governor-General has approved of the Bill, or, as the phrase goes, when the **Royal Assent** has been given to it, the Bill becomes an Act, and, from that time forward, it is part of the law of the land, which you and I are bound to obey until it is altered. Now that you understand how carefully laws are made, and how they have to be considered and approved by the chosen representatives of the people, you will see how wrong it is to try to evade or break the law — still more how wrong it is to try to alter it by force.

The Law Must Be Obeyed.

6. As the laws are made by all for the benefit of all, anybody who tries by force to break them or set them aside is a **traitor**, not to the King only, but to his country, and to **his countrymen** who have made the law which he is bad enough to break. Therefore, you see, it must always be wrong to use force or violence or to disobey the law.

7. I do not mean that all the laws that are made are good ones, or that we shall be wise in always resting content with the laws as they are. On the contrary, there are many laws which are bad in themselves, and there are many others which become useless or old-fashioned as times change.

8. But if a law be bad, or if it be no longer needed, there is one way, and one way only, in which it can rightly be altered or got rid

6   For example, a Bill containing provisions inconsistent with treaty obligations entered into by Britain with other powers, or a Bill affecting the royal prerogative.

of; that is, by persuading the majority of voters that it is bad or out of date, and getting them, through their members of Parliament, to change it or to do away with it. **In a free country, a law must be obeyed until it is altered.** It can only be altered by Act of Parliament. Every man who tries to alter it by any other means is a traitor to his country.

CHAPTER V.
HOW THE LAWS ARE CARRIED OUT.

> "Every purpose is established by counsel."
>
> — *Proverbs xx. 18.*

XII. GOVERNMENT DEPARTMENTS.

1. YOU have heard that the **country is governed by Parliament**; that is to say, that Parliament makes the law by which we are all governed. But when laws are made, there is still something to be done before they can be of much use, and that is that they should be put into practice.

2. In order to make sure that the laws are put into practice, and that all the arrangements made by Parliament are carried out in the best way, a large number of persons are employed in what are called the **Departments** (Commonwealth and State). These persons are called **Public Officers**, and to enter the **Public Service**, everyone has to pass an examination to show that he is fitted for the work that he or she has to do. This was not always so. At one time, places were given not to the cleverest or most deserving, but to those who had powerful friends to help them. It is a very good thing that the change has been made, for it is most important that the work of the country should be done in the best possible way by those who are most fitted by their knowledge and industry to do it.

3. At the head of each Department is a **Minister**, who is a mem-

ber of Parliament.[7] It is the Minister's business to see that everything goes right in his Department, and that all things are done which may be necessary for properly carrying on the particular work with which he is charged. The Ministers, as a body, form the **Government, Ministry, Cabinet, Administration**, or **Executive** (as it is variously called), which I mentioned before as occupying, with its supporters, the benches on the right of the Speaker. The **executive power**, formally vested in the Governor-General in the case of the Commonwealth, or in the Governor in the case of a State, is exercised through the Ministry, which depends upon the **support of the majority in the Lower House**, and, if it cannot retain their confidence, loses office. As regards **legislation** also, most of the **Bills** that become law are brought in by members of the Ministry. The Ministers of the Federal Government work under a chief called the **Prime Minister**, and the Ministers of the State Governments under a **Premier**.

4. I must glance now at the several Departments of the Federal and State Governments, and tell you a little about their duties. The **Federal Departments** are **seven** in number.

The Departments of the Commonwealth Government.

5. As under our Constitution or system of government there could not be Ministers without a Parliament, we may place first the **Minister for Home Affairs**, whose chief duty is to supervise the arrangements necessary for the **election** of the members of a Parliament.

6. The most important Minister, however, is the **Treasurer**, in whose care is the Treasury, where the books containing a record of

---

7   This is so in regard to the Federal Government, and usually so in regard to the State Governments. Of the Ministers, one or two only are, as a rule, members of the Upper House.

GOVERNMENT OFFICES, ADELAIDE.

(ERNEST GALL, ADELAIDE.)

all **moneys received** and **paid out** are kept. You will learn more of the duties of a Treasurer when I come to treat of the State Treasurer.

7. The greater part of the **revenue** collected in accordance with the will of the Commonwealth Parliament is obtained by taxes on goods brought into the country, and upon certain articles—mainly spirits and tobacco—manufactured here. To control the collectors of customs duties at the various ports and also the excise[8] officers, there is a **Minister of Trade and Customs**, who is also entrusted with the supervision of ports and harbours.

8. In order that we may be able to trade freely with other nations, we must be at peace; and to be allowed to remain at peace, a nation must be ready for war. The **Minister of Defence** is charged with the heavy duty of keeping Australia in such a condition that an enemy invading it would be repelled. He is concerned, therefore, with the building and arming of **forts** at the entrances to our harbours, with the equipment and arming of our **defence forces**, including our cadet corps. Later, I shall tell you more about what is being done in the matter of the defence of our country against an invader.

9. Another Minister whose duties have some relation to those of the Minister of Defence is the **Minister of External Affairs**. When occasion arises, he communicates with the State Governments, sees that the laws in reference to immigration are obeyed, and deals with all questions affecting our relations with foreign countries.

10. To advise the Government in matters of **law**, there is an **Attorney-General**. Business connected with the High Court is part of his charge.

11. The **Postmaster-General** has the pleasant duty of working a Department that is **revenue-producing**. He has under his supervision the post and telegraph offices and the telephone system.

---

8   An inland duty levied upon certain articles grown or manufactured in the country. The word is apparently derived from the Latin *excisum*, cut off.

THE POST OFFICE

12. Wonderful are the arrangements by which letters and telegrams can be sent safely not only from one end of Australia to the other, but to the United Kingdom, to China, to India, to America, and to almost every corner of the globe.

13. It is hard to understand how enormous is the quantity of letters, etc., which are sent safely each year. Australians and New Zealanders stand, as letter writers, in the front rank among nations. In 1907, the number of letters, etc., that went through the post in the Commonwealth and the Dominion was between four and five hundred millions, averaging more than eighty for each inhabitant. In that year, also, orders and postal notes for nearly £9,000,000 were issued or paid by Post Office officials. In another chapter, I shall tell you something of the savings banks which, in most of the States, are **managed by the Post Office, and which are a great help** to all those who are wise enough to wish to save money for a rainy day. But now I will only tell you one or two things which will interest you about the stamping and posting of letters.

14. Anyone can now send a letter from the United Kingdom to any part of the British Empire **for a penny**. Many years ago, things were very different, every letter costing from sixpence to a shilling; and very many people were unable to afford to write letters at all.

15. It was not till 1840 that **Sir Rowland Hill** first saw that not only could letters be carried for a penny without loss, but that by making it so easy for everyone to write and receive letters, the numbers of stamps used and letters sent would be enormously increased. By persuading the British Parliament to try his plan, he conferred a very great boon not only upon the people of the United Kingdom, but also upon the inhabitants of countries about which he had probably not given a thought.

16. I am tempted to tell you about one other Englishman who did great service to us all by his work at the Post Office. I refer to

THE GENERAL POST OFFICE, SYDNEY.

(STAR PHOTO CO., SYDNEY)

Mr. Fawcett, the blind Postmaster-General, who died in 1884. I mention him in the first place because, by the many improvements he made in the working of the Post Office, he has earned the right to be remembered as a good and useful Minister; and in the second place, I mention him because, both by his life and by his work, he gave an example to all his countrymen of what may be done, under the greatest difficulties and the most terrible afflictions, by one who is devoted to the service of his country.

The Departments of the State Governments

17. The **Treasurer** (called in New South Wales, Queensland, and Western Australia, the **Colonial Treasurer)** of a State, like the Treasurer of the Commonwealth, is the most important Minister of the Government, and the office is usually held by the **Premier**. The prosperity of the State depends, in no small measure, on the satisfactory management of the **public funds**. In his **Budget speech**, which is delivered every year, the Treasurer makes an announcement concerning the results of the expenditure of the public money during the preceding year, and what the Ministry proposes to spend during the year to come; he indicates the taxes he will ask Parliament to impose, and states whether it will be necessary or advisable to borrow money in the near future.

18. The people of the various States own the railways within their boundaries, and, therefore, there is in each a **Minister of Railways** to regulate the vast army of workers connected with them. He is responsible to Parliament for the working of his Department, and for the expenditure of the funds placed at its disposal.

19. Every year the Parliament of each State votes a large sum of money—considerably more than half a million pounds in New South Wales and Victoria—to be spent in building and repairing schools, in paying teachers, and in supplying them with material with which to do their work. The **Minister** (or, as he is called in New South

Wales and Queensland, the **Secretary) of Public Instruction** has to see that this money is properly spent, that the law compelling children to attend school regularly is carried out, and, generally, that the progress of education—both primary and secondary—in the State is satisfactory.

20. The **Chief Secretary** controls public libraries and museums, and the prisons and lunatic asylums. The police force is also under his supervision in Victoria, but under that of the Minister for Justice in New South Wales.

21. The **Attorney-General** is the head of the legal staff and the adviser of the Government in matters of law. He represents the Crown in cases brought into court.

22. In some of the State Governments, there is a **Minister of Labour**, one of whose duties—his chief duty—is to see that the provisions of the **Factory Act** are carried out.

23. In one or other of the several State Governments, there are other Ministers who have portfolios, that is, manage Departments, such as the **Minister of** (or, as the title runs sometimes, **Secretary for) Lands**, of **Public Works**, of **Public Health**, of **Agriculture**. Their titles indicate their duties as far as you need to learn at present.

XIII. THE COLONIAL OFFICE, LONDON

1. It is interesting to know how the Governor-General, the State Governors, and their Ministers keep touch with the King and his advisers, or, in other words, **how the Imperial connection is maintained**. This is done through the Colonial Office in London—an office of great importance, and one to which many difficult questions are sent for consideration and settlement.

2. The member of the British Ministry at the head of the Colonial Office is called the **Secretary of State for the Colonies**, and it is his business to see to everything that concerns the Colonies, including, of course, Australia. He gives instructions to our Governors,

THE GOVERNMENT HOUSE, BRISBANE.

receives through them communications from the various Governments of which they form a part, and supplies information to the British Parliament on all questions relating to the Commonwealth and the States.

How Australia is represented in Britain

3. If you went to London, you would certainly not miss visiting that great building about which so many historical memories cling—Westminster Abbey. When going to see it, you might pass along Victoria Street, and you would see, if you looked carefully, the inscriptions:

"AGENT-GENERAL FOR QUEENSLAND."
"AGENT-GENERAL FOR TASMANIA."
"AGENT-GENERAL FOR WESTERN AUSTRALIA."

4. These would serve to remind you that a man of ability from each of the Australian States is maintained in London to consult about the affairs of his State with the King's Ministers, to transact business for it, to express its views on public questions, and to give information to persons who think of emigrating or who wish to find a profitable investment for their money. In 1909, a **High Commissioner** for Australia was appointed to represent the Commonwealth.

5. What a splendid system links the New Country with the Old—the **High Commissioner** and six **Agents-General** in London representing the Governments of the Commonwealth and the States, the **Governor-General** and **Governors** representing the Imperial Government!

CHAPTER VI.
OUR LITTLE PARLIAMENTS.

"The greatest trust between man and man is the trust of giving counsel."

— *Bacon.*

XIV. LOCAL GOVERNMENT.

1. YOU have heard about Parliament, how it is elected, and how it makes laws for the whole country. You have seen also how the Ministers, and those who are put under them in the different offices, carry out the laws which are made by Parliament.

2. But besides the laws that are required for the Commonwealth, and are the same for all parts of it, and those that are required for each State, and are the same for all parts of it, there are other regulations which have to be made for the government of different parts of the State. These are not the same in all respects, for the wants of one place may differ from those of another, and the people who live on the spot will know best what the wants of each place are.

3. The Parliaments of each State have, therefore, passed laws giving to the inhabitants of certain areas the right to elect **a little Parliament or Council** of their own to do the work required for the proper government of their particular district. None of these little Parliaments can make any law or rule which is contrary to a law made by the Parliament of the State, and they can only concern themselves with such matters as are entrusted to them by Parliament.

4. During the first fifty years or so of Australia's history, the central Governments themselves carried out all public improvements. It was

in **1842** that local government was first introduced into the colony of New South Wales, when **Municipal**[9] **Councils** were established in Sydney and Melbourne.[10] Adelaide, indeed, the capital of South Australia—a colony founded in 1836 quite apart from New South Wales—had its Council two years earlier, but it was not a success, and was dissolved, to be renewed, however, some years afterwards.

5. The system of local government has been steadily extended, and now is widespread. For instance, the whole of Victoria, the most thickly populated State, is divided into municipalities, and the Councils, whose members receive no payment, discharge their duties with credit and success. In those parts of the other States where the people are widely scattered, whatever public improvements are made—chiefly the formation of roads—have still to be carried out by the central Governments.

How Councillors are Elected.

6. The members of these local governing bodies, which are known by various names, such as **Municipal Corporations, District Councils, Shire Councils**, and **Roads Boards**, are elected in much the same way as members of Parliament. But there is this important difference: in the case of choosing a member to sit in any of the Lower Houses of Parliament, one man or woman has one vote only; but in electing a Municipal Councillor, a person who owns a small amount of property is allowed to have one vote, while another who owns a large amount has votes in proportion up to a certain limit. There is wisdom in this provision, for the idle and negligent should not have a voice in the business of the Corporation equal to that of the

9 Latin *munia*, official duties, functions; *capere*, to take. In ancient Italy, a *municipium* was a town that possessed the right of Roman citizenship, but was governed by its own laws.

10 Melbourne was, at that time, the chief town in the Port Phillip District, a part of New South Wales. In 1851, the Port Phillip District became a separate colony under the name of Victoria.

THE TOWN HALL, SYDNEY.

diligent and thrifty who have accumulated property, and would lose a great deal if the management of affairs were in incapable hands. The privilege of voting is not confined to **property holders**; it is also given to **tenants** and **lodgers**.

7. The number of members in a municipal body varies according to the size or the importance of the area of country represented by it. A shire or district, with its two or three thousand people, will have no more than, say, nine members, while the large cities have two or three times that number.

8. Care is taken that the whole of a municipality shall receive its fair share of attention by dividing it into parts—**wards, ridings**, or whatever they may be termed—and allowing the ratepayers in each part to elect their own representative or representatives.

9. The Councillors hold fortnightly or monthly meetings in some central place, and every year a chairman or presiding officer is elected, either by the ratepayers or, as is more commonly the case, by the Councillors themselves. If the year's revenue of the Council reaches a certain amount, he is called the **Mayor**[11]; if it does not, he must, as a rule, be content with some such title as **President** or **Warden**. All the members of the Councils of Sydney and Brisbane are called **Aldermen**[12], and in some of the other Councils—for example, those of Melbourne, Adelaide, and Hobart—a small proportion of the members are so styled.

10. A fixed number of Councillors retire every year[13], but any retiring Councillor may present himself for re-election. A Council is thus a continuous body, and while changes can be made in its

11 The power to confer the title of Lord Mayor on their presiding officer was granted to the Corporations of Sydney and Melbourne in 1902.
12 *Alderman* is from an Anglo-Saxon word *caldor*, an elder, combined with *man*.
13 All the aldermen of the Sydney Municipal Council retire at the end of every two years.

personnel, yet they cannot be hasty or sweeping, which is generally an advantage.

11. Of the principal permanent officers of a Council, the first in importance is the **Clerk** or **Secretary**. He keeps the books, attends to all correspondence, and in connection with the meetings, notifies the members, draws up the business paper, and takes minutes of the proceedings. Then comes the **Treasurer**, who is entrusted with the safekeeping of the Council's revenue and the disbursement of money upon orders made by the proper authority; the **Rate-collector**, who sends out notices of money due, collects it, and compiles the *Roll of Ratepayers*; and the **Engineer** or **Surveyor**, who estimates the cost and draws plans of works the Council has under consideration.

What the Councils Do.

12. The **chief business** of a Council is to construct and maintain roads[14] and footpaths, to make provision for lighting the streets, to see that drainage is attended to and rubbish removed, and, in large towns, to secure the carrying out of laws[15] relating to the building of houses, and to do many other things for the comfort and convenience of the people it represents. Councils also regulate markets, pounds, slaughtering-houses, places of recreation, charitable institutions, and act as Boards of Health, and sometimes as Water Trusts.

A Council's Revenue.

13. To carry out the work entrusted to them, municipal bodies, of course, require **money**. Part of this they obtain by means of rates, which, by the law of the State, cannot be more than a certain amount in every £ of the annual value of a person's property.

14   The main roads have, for the most part, been constructed by the central Government of each State, and are, in many cases, still maintained by it.

15   Power is given to a Council to make by-laws (local laws), which, after they have received the approval of the Government of the State, must be obeyed within the boundaries of the area under that Council.

14. Thus, if a man owns a house that is assessed by the valuer for the municipality at £50 a year, his rates will amount to £3 6s. 8d. a year, if the **general rate** is a shilling in the £ and the **lighting rate** 4d. But this may not be his only outlay for rates. He may have to pay a **sanitary rate** and a **water rate** (though perhaps not to the Council) calculated upon the annual value of his property.

15. Fees for licences of various kinds form another source of revenue.

16. Most of the municipalities are also **assisted by the State Governments**, which supplement the amount of the rates collected, in accordance with a fixed scale (giving, in some cases, £ for £), and also **make grants** to aid them in carrying out special works that are of national benefit.

17. It is thought to be a **good thing** to save the central Government in this way from having to attend to small matters at a long distance from the capital. In most cases, also, the work is done better and more cheaply by the people on the spot, and it makes people realise better how they are governed.

Boards and Trusts.

18. In addition to the Councils of the type about which I have been speaking, and of which there are many hundreds throughout the Commonwealth, there are also, in most of the States, bodies of men known as **Boards** and **Trusts**, which have power given them by Parliament to carry out certain work within a definite area that usually includes several municipalities. Such a piece of work, for example, as the sewering of a city and its suburbs, may be handed over to a Board, which represents all the people interested and is given power to impose a rate. Then there are **Water Supply Trusts** concerned with supplying a town with water, and **Irrigation Trusts** appointed to manage the distribution of water to crops and orchards from reservoirs constructed by the Government. The means of

extinguishing fires in a city is likely to be better organised by a Board which has that for its sole duty than by the City Council with many other things to look after; and so we have **Fire Brigade Boards**.

The True Work of Councils.

19. The work of the Councils is, in one way, very different from the work of Parliament, for, though part of their business is to make laws and regulations, by far the most important thing they have to do is to **carry out the laws already made**. For this reason, it is very important that only those persons should be elected to the Councils who have experience in business and who are hard workers. A man who only makes speeches and gives no attention to business is even more useless in a Council than in Parliament itself.

XV. FEDERAL, STATE, AND MUNICIPAL GOVERNMENT: A REVIEW

1. Now, perhaps, as you have read a great deal about the Federal, State, and Municipal Governments, your ideas may be somewhat confused, so I have hit upon a device to give them definiteness in regard, at any rate, to the leading facts.

2. On the next page you will see a map that should interest you very much. Look at it, and think first of the **Federal Parliament**, with its two Houses—the Senate and the House of Representatives. Well, the **whole State** of Victoria, of which a part is represented on the map, is polled as **one electorate for the Senate**; and the people of full age (men and women) within the area bounded off thus and named *Indi (an Electoral Division)* return a **member** to the **House of Representatives**. On the map are shown also portions of other Electoral Divisions for the same House, namely *Echuca, Mernda, and Gippsland*.

3. Now turn your attention to the **State Parliament**, with its two Houses—the Legislative Council and the Legislative Assembly. The

MAP OF A PART OF THE STATE OF VICTORIA.

voters within the area enclosed by the heavy black line (an *Electoral Province*) elect a member for the former, while those in the parts of it enclosed by x X x (*Electoral Districts*), namely *Benambra, Ovens, Wangaratta, Benalla*, and *Upper Goulburn*, each send a member to the latter. To facilitate the holding of an election, these electorates are also cut up into divisions, the names of which you will see are printed on the map in upright letters with boundaries indicated thus —, and in sloping letters with boundaries indicated thus, respectively.

4. Lastly, the words in the south of the map—*Shire of Oxley, Shire of Bright*—are intended to bring your thoughts from the State to the **Municipality**. The whole area of the State represented on the map is portioned off into *Municipal Districts*—boroughs and shires—each having its own Council. Their boundaries, almost without exception, coincide with those of the State electorates and their divisions.

5. If you call to mind now the low qualification necessary to secure a vote, you will see that there are **very few men** living in that part of Victoria represented on the map (and the same may be said of almost all the settled parts of Australia and Tasmania) who **do not possess the right to share in the government** of the Commonwealth, the State, and the Municipality.

6. It is to be regretted that interest in political questions is wanting to such an extent in many people that they will not take the trouble to record their votes.

CHAPTER VII.
LAW AND JUSTICE.

"In the first class I place the judges as of the first importance.
It is the public justice that holds the community together."

— Burke.

XVI. THE OLD PLAN AND THE NEW.

1. In all civilised countries in the world, there are **Courts of Justice
and Judges** whose duty it is to decide disputes between people who
are unable to agree about their rights, and to try and to punish those
who break the law.

2. In savage and uncivilised countries only are there no judges to
be found; in such places disputes are still settled by force, those who
are strongest taking what they desire from others who are too weak
to resist. In the early history of England, you will find a time when
the same bad plan was followed, and when, instead of bringing their
claim before a magistrate or a judge, men chose rather to adopt—

"The good old way, the ancient plan—
To let him take who hath the power,
And let him keep who can."

3. You will not require to think very long before you see that
this "good old way" was in reality a very bad way. In fact, so long
as people try to settle their own quarrels and their own disputes in
the way they themselves think right, there will never be peace and
contentment in a country.

The "Bad" Old Way.

4. And so it is, too, with the punishment of those who commit crimes. There was a time in England when, if one man killed another, the friends and relations of the murdered man used to arm themselves and attack the home of the murderer, and try to take his life. Of course, it sometimes happened that the friends of the criminal were more powerful than those of the injured man, and that the party which had right on their side were beaten, and matters became even worse than they were before.

5. And, indeed, whichever side was successful, the result was bad for those who themselves undertook to revenge injuries which they or their friends had suffered, and forgot the two great rules which at all times we should bear in mind:—

Two Rules.

First—*"That no one should be a judge in his own cause.*

And, secondly—*"That no one should take the law into his own hands."*

6. In order that these two important rules should be observed, the plan has been adopted in all civilised countries of appointing certain persons to hear and decide upon all disputes, and to try all offenders. These persons, as you know, are **judges and magistrates**, to whom is given power to give decisions and to award punishments.

The Judges

7. It is necessary that the judges should do their work without fear or favour, and with perfect fairness. For this reason, they are **appointed for their whole life**, and can only be dismissed for bad conduct, when a request that this course should be followed is made by both Houses of Parliament to the Governor-General in the case of a judge of the High Court of Australia, or to a Governor in the case of other judges.

8. By being thus appointed for life, the judges are more likely to be perfectly fair, for they can look forward to no further favour, and can give all their thought and all their strength to doing their own work well, without having to think of how they may best provide for themselves, as they would have to do in case they were made to give way to other men after they had served for a few years only.

The Work of the Judge

9. It is not the business of the judges to *make* the law; that, you remember, is done by Parliament. But what they have to do is to *decide whether the laws that Parliament has made have been broken*, and whether the rules Parliament has approved of have been obeyed.

10. Besides this, they have to say **what punishment shall be given** to those who break the law. But you must not suppose that the judge or the magistrate can give what punishment he likes; on the contrary, he is only allowed to punish each crime according to the rules laid down by law. For instance: let us suppose that two men break into a house and rob the people to whom the house belongs.

11. When it is proved that they are guilty of the crime, the law says they may both be punished by being sent to prison for a long term of years. It may turn out, however, that one of the two men has often been sent to prison before, and that the other has always had a good character, but has been led away by his comrade. Then the judge will send the one to prison for the whole term the law allows, but the other he will probably send to prison for six months only, in the hope that he may profit by the lesson and lead an honest life afterwards. So you will see that the judge has the right to vary the punishment, but he can never punish any man beyond what the law permits.

THE LAW COURTS, MELBOURNE.

The Jury

12. I have been talking to you all this time about the judges only; but, as I dare say most of you know, in a court of justice, besides the judge, there is generally the **Jury**. What is the jury? What is the use of it? And what does it do?

13. When a prisoner is to be tried, twelve men are chosen by lot out of a long list of people living in the neighbourhood, and it is their business to hear all that is said for and against the prisoner, to listen to what the judge tells them about the law, and then to say whether they think the prisoner is "**guilty or not guilty.**" These men are called **jurymen**; and every Australian has the right to be **tried by a jury** in all cases where he is charged with a crime of a serious nature[16].

The Use of the Jury

14. The great use of a jury is to make sure that no prisoner shall be punished unjustly or let off unjustly, only because the persons who hear his case are his enemies or his friends. You will see that if the judge only were to decide, it is possible that he might be led to do so unfairly because he disliked the prisoner, or because he was a friend of the man whom the prisoner had injured, or for some other personal reason. But when twelve men are taken by chance out of a great number, it is very unlikely—indeed, it is almost impossible—that they should all be friends or enemies of the prisoner. It is much more likely that they will be fair to both sides. And in this way, juries help the cause of right and justice.

15. When a man is tried by a jury in Australia, it is the rule that *all the jurymen* must be agreed before he is pronounced "guilty" or "not guilty." In Scotland, the jury numbers fifteen, and the rule is that *the majority decides*—that is, if eight out of the fifteen think

16   In addition to juries in Criminal trials, there are, sometimes, special juries to decide questions of damages in Civil cases.

that the prisoner has committed the crime with which he is charged, then he is declared guilty.

16. The decision of the jury is called its "**verdict**"; and when the verdict has been given, then it is the turn of the judge to pronounce **the sentence** and to fix **the punishment**. In the next chapter, I shall give you an account of a trial before a judge and jury, and shall try to explain to you the rules by which the work of justice is done.[17]

17   In many cases, however, prisoners are tried by a judge only, without the help of a jury, and British judges are upright men who can be trusted to do justice without fear or favour.

CHAPTER VIII—PART I
THE TRIAL

"The law is no respecter of persons."

XVII. MAXIMS

1. I AM now going to give you an account of a trial in a court of justice before a judge. But first, you must learn some of the great rules which are observed in courts of justice wherever British law is administered. They are four in number, and are as follows:—

i. Everyone is equal before the law.

ii. Every man is held to be innocent until he is proved to be guilty.

iii. No man can be tried twice for the same offence.

iv. All courts of justice are open to the public.

To these four great rules you should add the other two which you have already learnt. They are:

v. No one is a judge in his own cause.

vi. No one has the right to take the law into his own hands.

2. Now we have got our rules, let us see how they work.

The Crime

Let us suppose that a robbery has been committed—that some silver spoons have been stolen from a house during the daytime.

3. The police find out first all they can about the theft. They ask questions from the owner of the house; they examine all the people who were about at the time of the robbery. At last they learn enough

to make them suspect a particular man, and they go to a justice of the peace or a magistrate for a **warrant**, or order, to allow them to take him prisoner; for, unless they see a man actually committing a crime, not even the police can take him prisoner without such a warrant.

4. The next thing that happens is that the prisoner is himself brought before a justice of the peace or a magistrate, and if it appears that the police have fair reason to think that the prisoner is the real thief, he will be *committed for trial*; that is to say, he will be sent back to prison to wait until the judge comes to try him. Where only small crimes have been committed, the magistrates may themselves try the prisoner, and if they find that he be guilty, they may send him to prison; but all the more serious crimes are tried by the judges.

5. When the prisoner is sent back to prison to wait for his trial, he is only shut up and kept safe; he is not made to do hard work like those who have been tried and found guilty, for, as I told you in Rule II, *"Every man is held to be innocent until he is proved to be guilty."*

The Accusation

6. After a time, the prisoner is brought before a judge in the capital of the State, or in some large town which is visited periodically by a judge. But, first of all, the cases of all prisoners are brought under the notice of the **Attorney-General of the State**, whose business it is to say whether or not there is any real proof that those accused are guilty of the crimes with which they are charged. If he thinks the case has been trumped up, or that no one can really say whether an accused person did what he or she was charged with or not, then he has the right to stop the case going to the judge at all, and the prisoners are set free.

The Court

7. But if, as usually happens, he thinks that, at any rate, there is some reason for believing that the police are right, and that they have got hold of the real criminal, then he sends the case to be tried

by the judge and jury in court. At last, the name of the prisoner who is accused of robbing the house is called out, and he is brought into court.

8. In front of him sits the judge in his wig and robes, and on one side of the judge sits the jury, twelve in number, chosen by lot out of a large number of persons living in the neighbourhood. The prisoner himself is put into the **dock**, where he is guarded by policemen.

9. But this is not all; for besides the judge, the jury, and the prisoner, you will see two or three men in wigs and black gowns sitting opposite the judge. They are the **lawyers**—those whose business it is to show what the case is against the prisoner, and to prove, if they can, that he is guilty, on the one hand; and those whose business it is to defend the prisoner, and to try to prove him innocent, on the other. The first are called **counsel for the Crown,** which means the Government, or **counsel for the prosecution**; the second are the **counsel for the prisoner**.

XVIII. THE LAWYERS

1. You will, perhaps, think it strange that it should be necessary to have lawyers at all, and that it would be better to let the prisoner speak for himself, and to let the people who saw him commit the crime speak against him. But this would not really be the best way. It has been found that justice is best done when this plan of having men who know the law to ask questions on both sides is adopted. In this way, everything that can be said against the prisoner, and everything that can be said in his favour, is said; and when both sides have done all they can, the jury and the judge are able to make up their minds as to where the real truth lies.

2. Sometimes, indeed, a prisoner likes to speak for himself without the help of any lawyer, and he always has the right to do so. But, in the greater number of cases, he does not use this right; and he is wise in not doing so, for few people, whether they are innocent or guilty,

IN COURT: THE EXAMINATION OF A WITNESS BY COUNSEL

are able to keep their thoughts quite clear when they are brought up in court and accused of a crime. Moreover, it is difficult even for clever and educated people to ask and answer all the questions which may be necessary, and they are much more likely to do themselves harm than good by trying.

3. The rest of the court is filled up with people who wish to hear the trial; and if there is room, you or I may go in and stop there as long as we behave ourselves respectfully and quietly, for *"All courts of justice are open to the public."*

The Judge

4. But before I begin to tell you about the trial, I want you to notice one or two things in reference to the court. First of all, when the judge comes in, everybody rises from his seat as a mark of respect, and everyone, no matter who he may be, takes off his hat and keeps it off as long as the judge is present.[18] This is right, for the judge, who is doing his work for the good of all the people, deserves our respect; and there is no one in the land who ought not to feel, and to show that he feels, this respect, for *everyone is equal before the law."*

The Story of Judge Gascoigne and Prince Henry

5. Those of you who remember your English history will know the story of **Judge Gascoigne and Prince Henry**. It is a good lesson to us of the duty of the judge to make the law respected, and of the duty of every man, rich and poor alike, to submit to the law. Prince Henry, who afterwards became **Henry V. of England**, was in his youth a wild scapegrace, accustomed to live with bad companions, and often mixed up in unworthy brawls.

6. One day it happened that one of the Prince's companions was brought before Chief Justice Gascoigne for the commission of

18   Police in uniform do not remove their helmets.

some crime. The young Prince, angry at his friend's capture, and believing that, as a son of the king and heir to the throne, he would be able to terrify the Chief Justice, appeared in court, and, with threatening words, laid his hand upon his sword, and ordered the judge to release the prisoner.

7. But Gascoigne was mindful of the duties of his office, and remembered that **the law is no respecter of persons**. So far from releasing the prisoner, he gave orders that Henry himself should be committed to gaol for daring to insult one of the judges of the land. To prison, therefore, the Prince went, according to the story; and, to his credit, it is said that, so far from blaming the act of the judge, he recognised and honoured the courage and wisdom which Gascoigne had shown.

8. When his father, King Henry IV, was told of what had happened, he said, *"Happy is the king who possesses a judge so resolute in the discharge of his duty, and a son so willing to yield to the authority of the law."*

So true is it that justice which is not equal for all alike is no justice at all.

9. But let us get back to the trial and see what takes place.

The Jury

First of all, the jury are made to take an oath to *"well and truly try"* the question which is to come before them. Those who think that it is wrong to take **an oath** are allowed to **affirm**, or make **a solemn promise**, which, of course, is really quite as binding as the oath, and which it would be quite as wrong to break.

The Trial

10. Then the trial begins. First, the counsel for the prosecution tells the jury the history of the crime—why it is the prisoner is suspected of having committed it, and how he is going to *prove* that

IN COURT: THE EXAMINATION OF A WITNESS BY COUNSEL

he did. For everything must be proved, because, as you remember, *every man is held to be innocent until he is proved to be guilty*. So that, however sure the judge and jury might be that the prisoner were really guilty, the law would not allow them to condemn him unless what they thought were proved to be true.

The Witnesses

11. When the counsel has finished his speech, he begins to call his **witnesses**; that is to say, he calls and questions all the people who have seen the crime committed, or who have seen things which happened before or after it, and which make it likely that the prisoner was the real criminal. For instance, one witness may say that he saw the door of the house open just before the spoons were stolen. Another may say that he saw the prisoner running down the street just after. And a third may say that, on another day, the prisoner offered to sell him some silver spoons. Now, none of these things alone would show much, but taken all together they show a good deal.

12. You must notice, however, that no witness is allowed to speak about, or, as it is called, **to give evidence** about, that which he has only heard from others. It is what he has himself seen and what he knows himself that he is allowed to tell when he is giving evidence which may end in sending another man to prison.

13. It is well to remember this rule, and, indeed, we shall do well to make it a rule for ourselves, and to be very careful how we believe mere hearsay or report, whatever it may be about, and especially if it is anything to the discredit of others. The greatest injustice has often been done by believing evil too readily, and the law is very wise in laying it down as a rule that *hearsay evidence shall not be received*.

14. Each witness, as he comes forward, is made, like the jury-man, to take an oath, or else solemnly to affirm that he will **tell the truth, the whole truth, and nothing but the truth**; and if he intentionally tells more than the truth, or less than the truth, or

what is untrue, he commits a crime against law called **perjury**, which we sometimes speak of as **bearing false witness**; and for that crime he may be severely punished, for it is necessary that, above all things, truth, and truth only, shall be spoken in a Court of Justice.

XIX. THE PRISONER'S CASE

1. As soon as **the counsel for the prosecution** has finished questioning each witness, the counsel for the prisoner again questions him, in order to show, if possible, that what he has said is incorrect, or that he has said less or more than the witness really knows, or that he has left something out which is in the prisoner's favour. Then the first counsel asks a few more questions, so as to allow the witness to correct any mistakes he may have made, and then the next witness is called. This goes on till all the witnesses for the prosecution have been examined.

2. Then comes the turn of **the prisoner's counsel**; he calls witnesses favourable to his side. He may, for instance, call someone who proves that the prisoner was in another part of the town when the robbery was committed, or that the spoons he sold were the prisoner's own property, or anything else which helps to show that the prisoner is innocent. All these witnesses are **cross-examined** in their turn, just as the others were, only this time by the counsel for the prosecution; and, like them, they are also re-examined.

3. Then the prisoner's counsel makes a speech, in which he goes through all that has been said for and against the prisoner, and tries to show that what has been said in his favour is to be believed, and that what has been said against him is untrue. Last of all comes the speech of the counsel for the prosecution, who does the same thing, but puts matters in another light, so as to show the jury that, after all, the prisoner is guilty.

COUNSEL ADDRESSING A JURY ON BEHALF OF THE PRISONER

The "Summing-up" and Verdict

4. If matters stopped here, you may fancy that the poor jury would find it a very hard task to make up their minds after so much has been said on both sides; but luckily there is the judge to help them. It is now time for him to **"sum up"**; that is to say, to go through all that has been said on *both* sides, to guide the jury, to show them what evidence is important and what is unimportant, and to explain to them what the law says about the crime./

5. Then the jury consult together, and when they are agreed (see page 83), their leader, or **foreman**, is asked by the **Clerk of the**

Court to say whether the jury find the prisoner "*Guilty*" or "*Not guilty*." If the verdict is "*Guilty*," the judge will then sentence the prisoner to be sent to gaol, and to be kept to hard labour. If, on the other hand, the verdict is "*Not guilty*," then the prisoner will walk out of the court a free man; and whatever may happen, he will never be in danger of being charged again with the robbery, for "*No man can be tried twice for the same offence.*"

6. Such is the way in which a trial is conducted in a Court of Justice. From beginning to end, everything is done for the purpose of finding out the truth, the whole truth, and nothing but the truth — of letting the innocent go free, and of punishing the guilty.

Criminal and Civil Trials

7. I have now given you the account of the trial of a prisoner; you must not think, however, that all the time of the judges, the lawyers, and the juries is taken up with trying prisoners for crimes they have committed. There is another kind of work they have to do, which is nearly as important, and which takes up a great deal of their time.

8. When I told you that in old days, and in savage countries, men settled their disputes by force, and without justice or a fair trial, I spoke not only of revenging crimes, such as murder or theft, but of settling disputes as to people's rights, and deciding questions where two men claimed the same thing; and as we now use our judges and juries to punish criminals, so we also use them to settle disputes between those who cannot agree.

A Criminal Trial

9. Thus, if, as we have supposed, a man is accused of stealing, he is brought before a judge and tried for his crime; and that is called a *Criminal Trial*, and the court in which the trial takes place is called a *Criminal Court*.

A Civil Trial

10. But if, for instance, two men are unable to decide to whom a particular field or house belongs, or suppose that one man has bought a horse from another, and the buyer will not pay the money although he has got the horse, then, in each case, they will bring the matter before a judge, and he will try it, and will decide which is in the right — to whom the field belongs, or whether the man who bought the horse ought to pay the money. Such a trial as this is called a *Civil Trial*, and the court in which it is held is called a *Civil Court*.

11. I hope you will now see the difference between *criminal* and *civil* law. The first has to do with the punishment of all those who commit crimes against the law, such as murder, robbery, perjury, theft, and many other offences. The second has to do with the settlement of disputes about the rights of people who cannot agree; and these disputes may arise in hundreds of ways — about rent, about buying and selling, about doing harm to other people's property, about wills by which people leave their money after their death — in short, about every question of a man's rights which he cannot decide for himself.

12. All these may give rise to what are called **civil actions**; that is to say, trials for the purpose of finding out the rights of either side.

Our Courts

13. To give you an outline of the **judicial system** of each of the Australian States, or of even one of them, would take much space, and would prove of little interest or value to you. You should know, however, that there are, in all centres of population of any importance, honorary **justices of the peace** and salaried **magistrates** to decide both civil cases that do not involve much money, and criminal cases that are not very grave, and to send to a higher court those that appear to be of a serious nature.

14. Next above these *Courts of Petty Sessions*, as they are sometimes

called, are courts presided over by **judges**. They are known in the several States by such names as *General Sessions, Quarter Sessions, County, District, and Circuit Courts*, and are held in large towns at intervals during the year.

15. Then there is in each State a Supreme Court, consisting of a **Chief Justice** and several other **judges**. These judges try serious cases of crime, and, in addition, a suitor dissatisfied with a decision given against him in a lower court may appeal to them to have his case re-heard.

16. Lastly, under the Commonwealth Government, a Federal Supreme Court, called the *High Court of Australia* (which consists of a **Chief Justice** and two other **judges**), has been created. Appeals may be made to it from the decisions of the Supreme Courts of any of the States. Such appeals used formerly to go to the *Privy Council* in England, and, under certain conditions, there is still an appeal to that body both from the State Supreme Courts and from the High Court itself.

CHAPTER VIII – PART II.
THE AUTHORITY OF THE LAW.

"The majesty and power of law and justice."
– Henry IV., Part 2, Act 5, Scene 2.

XX. THE POWER OF THE JUDGES

1. I HAVE told you, and, indeed, you all know, that those who are proved before a Court of Justice to have broken the law are punished by being sent to prison. Those who have wilfully and unlawfully taken the life of another man are themselves put to death by the law.

2. It is a very terrible thing to be deprived of liberty even for a day; it is far more terrible to be shut up in prison for months, for years, and, in some cases, for a whole lifetime. For one man to take the life of another, even for the best reason in the world, is a very solemn thing. If anybody were to do any of these things out of revenge, they would be altogether bad, and nothing could excuse the man who took such a course.

Punishment

3. In the first place, revenge is altogether wrong and forbidden by our religion. In the second place, punishments that were intended only to hurt the person who had done wrong would be of very little good. The only way in which punishments can be made really useful is by taking care that they shall be an example and a warning to others, so that they may not commit the crime which the law

has condemned. To put it quite shortly, *all punishments should be preventive.*

4. In this way, the imprisonment to which a thief or a false witness is sentenced is useful in helping other people, and in warning them against crimes which lead to such a punishment.

5. And so we come round again to the explanation which I have given you so often before; and in the power of the judge to punish law-breakers, you will see another example of **work done by all for the good of all.**

Why We Should Honour The Judge

6. For the judge is really appointed by the people to do their work for them, and it is only because he is acting for all the people that he has any right to sentence and to punish.

7. When you understand this, you will understand why it is that everyone is bound to respect and to honour those who are chosen as judges, and why we should all support and help those whose business it is to carry out the law.

8. As you learnt in Chapter VII., **no one has a right to take the law into his own hands.** It is only when a man acts on behalf of all his countrymen that he has a right to do such a solemn thing as to condemn his fellow-men to death, to send them to gaol, or even to take them prisoners in the street.

The Policeman

9. And this is true not only of the judges on the bench, but it is true of every single man who helps to do the work of justice. You know that a **policeman** has the right to take up people who are disorderly in the streets, or who are seen stealing, or fighting, and that he may do a great many other things which you and I have no right to do.

10. Why is this? What is the difference between the policeman

and any other man? The difference is that the policeman has been appointed, just as the judge has been appointed, to do his work for the whole people of the country. If the people had not given him his authority, he would have had no more business than you or I have to lock up or interfere with others. But because he is thus, in a small way, doing his work in the cause of law and justice, we ought to respect his office, and to help him in his work, remembering that, without law and justice, we should be no better off than the worst savages.

11. In busy, crowded streets, too, the policeman renders great service to us by regulating the traffic, and visitors from other countries are generally very much struck by the sight of a policeman holding up his hand and keeping carts and cabs and carriages waiting while he lets people cross the road in safety.

Special Constables

12. To show you how true it is that the work which the policeman does is really done on behalf of all the people who have given him his authority, I will tell you what happens when the policemen are too few for the work which they have to do, or when the dangers which they have to meet in order to protect the public are very great.

13. At such times, the plan is followed of "**swearing in special constables**"; that is to say, of appointing ordinary citizens to help the police. When special constables have been appointed, they, too, have the right to arrest people and to help to keep order, just like policemen. It is usually in times of riot or great disturbance, as in Melbourne during the Maritime Strike in 1890, that they are appointed; and I have only spoken of them to show how really a policeman is doing work for you, and for me, and for all of us, which we should have to do for ourselves if he were not there.

CHAPTER IX.
BRITAIN'S NAVY AND ARMY.

"The blood of man should never be shed but to redeem the blood of man. It is well shed for our family, for our friends, for our God, for our country, for our kind—the rest is vanity; the rest is crime."

– Edmund Burke.

XXI. THE DEFENCE OF THE COUNTRY

1. ALL of you know something about **sailors** and **soldiers**; you know that their business is to protect the Country at home and to fight abroad if the need should arise. It would never do for me to tell you about the duties of a British citizen and to say nothing at all about those who are specially bound to fight for the Country. For really, the duty of a sailor or a soldier is the duty of **every man in the whole Empire.** It is more convenient that, during peace, only a few should give up their time and their thought to making the Country safe in time of war.

2. But we must never forget that the time may come when every man, rich and poor, high and low, might have to become a sailor or a soldier, and to risk his life for the defence of the Country. If the people of Britain were attacked, or there were a danger of their homes being invaded and their liberty interfered with, then the time would have come for every man strong enough to carry a rifle to join the Navy or the Army, and to give up his time and his money, and, if necessary, his life, in order that the enemy might be defeated.

Who Ought to Fight for the Country?

3. You will see farther on that, **by the law of the land, every man in Britain is obliged to fight for the Country** if it is in danger; but there is not much need of a law to make British citizens do this. When the time comes, if it ever does come, there will be plenty of defenders who will take up arms, not because the law compels them, but because they love their Country.

4. But, as you know, in times when there is no great danger, it is not necessary for every man to become a sailor or a soldier. Only those who specially choose to go to sea or to join the Army do so. When war comes, or when the rights of the subjects of the British Sovereign are threatened in any part of the world, they are ready to go and see that justice is done, and, if necessary, to use force to secure just treatment.

Voluntary Enlistment and Conscription.

5. In Britain, only those persons become sailors and soldiers who wish to do so; but in many countries it is otherwise.

6. In **France**, in **Germany**, in **Russia**, in **Austria**, and in **Italy**, every man is compelled to become a soldier or a sailor, whether he likes it or not, and is made to serve upon a ship of war or in a regiment for three or four years. This plan of making everybody a soldier or a sailor is called conscription. The British Navy and Army are recruited by **voluntary enlistment**; that is to say, they are made up only of those who wish to join them.

Frontiers.

7. It is a great cause for thankfulness that the people of Britain are able to be safe without conscription, and they owe their good fortune to their Country consisting of islands. Thus, unlike most foreign nations, they are not open to a sudden attack, for no enemy can pass their boundaries save by crossing the sea.

SHIPPING AT FREMANTLE.

8. It would amuse you to see some of those places in Europe where the division between two countries runs. By just crossing the road, you can go from Germany into France, or from Austria into Germany, and you would never be any the wiser until you found out that you had changed from one set of laws, one language, and one government to another.

9. Now, Australia is, in the matter of its boundaries, like Britain. Here are two pictures. One shows what the frontier line of Australia is like. It is a view of Fremantle, the nearest to Europe of the calling-places for European vessels. Before it stretches the Indian Ocean, which an enemy would have to traverse before he could reach it. Beautifully does one of Australia's poets, William Gay, refer to her ocean boundary:

> "From all division let our land be free,
>   For God has made her one; complete she lies
>   Within the unbroken circle of the skies,
> And round her indivisible the sea
> Breaks on her single shore."

There is an advantage in being "bound in by the triumphant sea."

10. And now look at the other picture: the little pillar with the word "ITALIA" written upon it. That is one of the boundary marks between **Switzerland** and **Italy**. On one side of the post, you are in the **Republic of Switzerland**, and governed by Swiss law; on the other side, you are in the **King-**

THE ITALIAN FRONTIER

dom of Italy, liable, if you are living in the country, to be made to serve as a soldier in the Italian army at Rome, at Naples, at Turin, and governed by laws made at Rome instead of at Berne.

11. So you see that a people whose country has such a frontier as no one can mistake have a good deal to be thankful for.

XXII. WHY THE NAVY COMES FIRST.

1. You will notice that I have spoken in this chapter of the "**Navy and Army**," and perhaps some of you will wonder why I did not talk of the Army and Navy, as people very often do. But, though it sounds a little strange to put the Navy first, it is quite right. For the Navy really ranks first, and if you were to be at a review where both sailors and soldiers were present, you would see that the sailors marched past before the soldiers.

2. Whenever the King, or one of his representatives, such as a Governor-General or a Governor, holds a review at which both soldiers and sailors are present, it is always easy to see whether it is the Navy or the Army which ranks first. One rule is always observed. The first to pass by are the bluejackets, or sailors, of the Navy, in their broad straw hats and white shirts. After them come the soldiers. This is really as it ought to be, for after all, it is the sea which is Britain's great defence, and it is those who protect her interests on the sea who ought to take the first place. The Navy is the first line of defence; that is to say, it is not till the Navy has been beaten that Britain's shores can be invaded by an enemy.

Britain's Sailors.

3. Let me, therefore, tell you something about British sailors and the ships in which they sail. In the whole British fleet, there are more than four hundred ships of war. Of these, about a dozen keep watch around the shores of Australasia (Australia, New Zealand, and the adjacent islands). The headquarters of this squadron are

in Port Jackson; but the vessels sometimes go to other ports; then many people visit them to look at the guns and other interesting things. Till its own fleet is of a certain strength, the Commonwealth Government helps to pay the cost of maintaining these ships, and many young Australians are being trained on board them[19].

4. Formerly, all ships were made of wood, and depended upon their sails only for getting from place to place. Now, however, all men-of-war are built of steel, and some of them are protected from the enemy's shot by very thick plates of iron or steel placed upon their sides. These are called "**ironclads.**" All of these vessels, large or small, are now steamers, and, by means of their engines, can go where they please, quite independently of the winds or the waves.

5. At the head of the fleet is an **Admiral**, and under him are **vice-admirals** and **rear-admirals**. Each ship is commanded by a **Captain**, and under him are **lieutenants**, **engineers**, **surgeons**, **boatswains**, **gunners**, **carpenters**, and a great number of other officers, each charged with special duties. The crew of each ship is made up of sailors, who are sometimes called "**bluejackets**," and of **engineers and stokers** to look after the machinery.

The Marines.

6. Nor must I forget to mention the **Marines**. On every ship, there is a certain number of men who belong to the **Royal Marines**. These men are trained like soldiers, but they go to sea in ships like sailors, and when it is necessary, they are sent from the ships to fight on land. The Royal Marines, though not exactly belonging either to the Navy or the Army, have fought bravely for their country in every part of the world, and have become justly famous.

7. Most of the bluejackets go into the Navy when they are quite boys, and this is a good plan, for to be a good sailor it is necessary to

19   *See also* "Australia's Defence Forces," p. 110.

H.M.S. EDWARD VII. AND TORPEDO DESTROYER.

SUB-LIEUTENANT AND BLUEJACKETS

be accustomed to the sea all one's life. The officers in the Navy also join it when they are boys, and before they can be advanced from one rank to another, they are examined in order to see that they know their work well, for it is most important that those who take charge of a great ship among the dangers of the ocean should be ready to do the right thing at the right time, and be prepared for the many sudden accidents that may befall from storms, or from the enemy.

What the Navy Does.

8. The ships for the Navy are chiefly built in the four great dock-yards—**Portsmouth, Plymouth, Chatham, and Pembroke.** When they are all ready, they are sent to sea. Some watch the coasts

of Britain; others, as you already know, go across the ocean to be on guard at various parts of the Empire.

9. Others, again, are sent to take care of the many thousands of merchant ships which, all the year round, are crossing the sea, conveying corn and wool and a hundred other things to the United Kingdom, or taking iron and coal and cloth from its mines and its mills to countries beyond the sea.

10. Some keep a look-out upon the slave ships, and others are employed in measuring the depth of the sea, in finding out the shapes of bays, peninsulas, etc., thus furnishing data for making the maps which are contained in your atlases. British sailors have much to do in time of peace; in time of war, we depend upon them for the safety of our lives and the freedom of our Country.

11. The history of Britain's Navy has been a very glorious one. Perhaps what has helped more than anything else to make it so is the fact that our greatest sailors, whether officers or seamen, have always made their chief thought the performance of their duty. "Duty" has been the great watchword of the Navy, and it was because he knew how great a power this simple word would have over the minds of his men that Admiral Nelson chose for his message to them, when they were about to engage in a deadly struggle with the French and Spaniards at Trafalgar, the famous words—**"England expects every man will do his duty."**

12. Thus you see that British sailors have a great deal to do in time of peace; and no one can tell how much may depend upon their skill and faithfulness in war-time.

XXIII. THE ARMY.

1. AND now I come to the Army. The history of the British Army, like that of the Navy, is a very famous one, and many a book has been written telling of the brave things which have been done by it. But what I have to do here is not to give you the history of the Army

(I hope you will read that elsewhere), but only to tell you how it is made up, and what it has to do.

Artillery—Cavalry—Infantry—Engineers.

2. The Army is divided into four branches—the **Artillery**, the **Cavalry**, the **Infantry**, and the **Engineers**. The artillery is composed of different **batteries**, the cavalry and infantry of **regiments**, the engineers of **troops** and **companies**. Besides these chief divisions, there are also doctors and hospital attendants to look after the sick and wounded, and a transport corps, a body of men whose business it is to carry provisions and stores of all kinds for the soldiers who are fighting.

3. The artillery have cannon, some drawn by four, and some by six horses.

4. The cavalry are armed with swords or lances, and, being mounted on horseback, are able to move quickly from place to place to get news and to prevent the Army from being surprised.

5. The engineers have a great deal of work to do; they make bridges, build forts, lay down telegraph wires, and do many other things which nowadays are necessary in time of war.

6. The infantry are foot soldiers, and are armed with rifles and bayonets.

7. At the head of each regiment, there is a **colonel**; and above the colonels, there are **generals**; and above them, again, is the **Inspector-General**.

Who Commands the Navy and Army.

8. In name, the **King**[20] is at the head of both the Navy and Army; but, as you may suppose, he does not take any active part in ordering them about or leading them. Still, it must be remembered that

20   The Defence Force in Australia is under the control of the Federal Parlia-

"The Crown" (as the King is sometimes called) is really the chief of both services.

9. But, of course, there would be neither soldiers nor sailors if there were no money to pay them with, and money can only be got, as I told you, by taxes voted by Parliament. So, however much the Crown wanted to use the Fleet or the Army without consulting the whole people, it could not do it, because Parliament could refuse to vote the money to pay the sailors and soldiers.

10. I have told you this about the King, the Parliament, and the Army because, though it is not very important nowadays, there was a time when there was a real danger of the King using the Army to put down the people, or to do things which were unjust and contrary to law. Fortunately, it is certain the present King would never try to act against the law; but you will see that if a King or Queen of England should ever try to do so, the people have a way by which they can protect themselves.

ment, and the Governor-General, being the King's representative, is Commander-in-Chief. (See also "Government Departments," p. 49.)

NAVAL DEPOT, GARDEN ISLAND, PORT JACKSON.

STAR PHOTO CO., SYDNEY.

CHAPTER X.

XXIV. AUSTRALIA'S DEFENCE FORCES.

"If we desire to avoid insult, we must be able to repel it. If we desire to secure peace, it must be known that we are, at all times, ready for war."
— *From Washington's Fifth Annual Address* (1793).

A National Navy and Army.

IN the early years of this century, the feeling gained strength among Australians that, to protect their native land successfully against invasion, a better system of defence was necessary than was being provided by the voluntary enlistment of soldiers and the payment of an annual sum of money to the Mother-country for the provision of warships. In obedience to the will of the people, the Federal Parliament legislated to enable a **national navy** and **army** to be formed.

The Navy.

Australia's **first line of defence** is her **Navy**, and a large addition is being made to the vessels the Commonwealth at present possesses. When this squadron is thought to be strong enough, the warships at present maintained on the Australian coast by agreement with the British Government (*see* page 104) will be withdrawn. The Australian Squadron will form a **Division of the Imperial Fleet**, ready not only to defend the shores of Australia, but also to help Great Britain when required, and to take a share in the defence of the Empire. There should be no lack of men to form the **Permanent**

Naval Forces required to work the ships and act as instructors, for a certain, continuous, and honourable career will be open to young Australians; and, added to that, there will be the pride born of the knowledge that they are engaged in the defence of their own homes. The conditions that have been provided for the training of boys who desire to become either officers or ordinary seamen are attractive. Further, of those liable to be trained as Senior Cadets (as explained later), such a number as is required will be chosen for training in the Naval Forces, passing, after cadet training, to the **Citizen Naval Forces**, and thence to the **Reserve**.

The Army.

By the operation of the Defence Act 1903–11, the **first army** formed under **compulsory training** in the British Empire will be brought into existence. It is there enacted that all the male inhabitants of Australia of certain ages (except those exempted for specified reasons) who have resided therein for six months, and are British subjects, are liable, under penalties of fine or imprisonment and ineligibility for employment in the Commonwealth Public Service in case of non-compliance, not only to serve within the boundaries of the Commonwealth and its Territories when called upon, but also to be **trained** as **Junior Cadets, Senior Cadets**, or **Citizen Forces**. While the army is being formed under this system, the present militia will be retained. There are no volunteers.

The Junior Cadets. All boys between the ages of **12 and 14** are required to go through a course of **physical exercises** (lasting for about 15 minutes during each school day) and **elementary marching drill**, and also to be trained in two of the following subjects:—Miniature Rifle Shooting, Swimming, Running Exercises in Organised Games, and First Aid. The Junior Cadets will be trained by their teachers. They are not to wear uniforms; but rifles will be issued on loan to such schools as have miniature rifle ranges. The time to be devoted to the training during the year must be at least **120 hours**, and there will be an inspection to test whether it is being carried out in a satisfactory manner.

The Senior Cadets.—During January of the year in which a lad reaches the age of **14 years**, he is required to **register** for **naval** and **military training**. To facilitate enrolment, organisation, and training, the Commonwealth has been divided into areas, in each of which there is an officer to organise and conduct the training. A doctor examines each lad, and those who are deemed fit are provided with arms, accoutrements[21], and uniforms, and enter upon their training from the 1st of July. The training of this force, at present about 110,000 strong, will consist of four whole-day parades of not less than 4 hours each, 12 half-days of not less than 2 hours, and 24 nights of not less than 1 hour. **Sixty-four hours must be served**. When there are 60 Senior Cadets in a school, they may receive their training there, if one of the officers of the detachment is a teacher at the school. There is a wise provision by which it is **forbidden** for Senior Cadets, when in uniform, or in any place used for military purposes, to have in their possession **intoxicating liquor** or **cigarettes**, and for anyone to have intoxicating liquor in his possession at any place where Cadets or members of the Citizen Forces up to the age of 25 years are being trained. On the 1st of July of the year in which they attain the age of 18 years, Senior Cadets will become members of the Citizen Forces.

The Citizen Forces.—Members of the Citizen Forces are required to undergo not less than 16 days' training (of which not less than 8 shall be in camps) each year until their **25th year**, and during their 26th year, to attend one muster parade. In specialist services (Artillery and Engineers), 25 days' training is required, of which 17 days must be in camps. Compulsory service ceases after the 26th year,

21   The additional items, equipment, or accessories that go with a particular role, activity, or way of life.

SENIOR MILITARY CADETS: FIRST INTERSTATE CHAMPIONSHIP COMPETITION, 1912.
PARADE OF TEAMS FROM NEW SOUTH WALES, VICTORIA,
QUEENSLAND, SOUTH AUSTRALIA, AND TASMANIA.

except in time of war, when it extends to the age of sixty years. Before receiving his discharge, however, each member must have twelve annual **entries** of **efficiency** or **exemption** in his record book, even if he takes till he is 30, 40, or 50 years of age to obtain them. The Citizen Forces will, when the scheme is complete, number about 120,000 men, organised in 92 battalions of **Infantry**, 56 batteries of **Artillery**, 28 regiments of **Light Horse**, **Garrison** Companies for defended forts, Field, Signal, Electric, and Submarine Companies of **Engineers**, together with the necessary departments and branches such as the **Army Medical Corps** and the **Army Service Corps**.

Instruction of the Permanent Forces

The Military College. — A college for the **training of officers** for the **Army** has been opened on the site of the capital of the Commonwealth. The students are chosen by examination, and do not pay fees. The course extends over four years; and graduates will be appointed to the **permanent force employed in the work of organisation and training.**

The Naval College. — There is being built, also, on Jervis Bay, the port of the capital, a college in which officers will be trained to carry out similar duties in connection with the **Navy**. As this college will not be ready for occupation for some time, the training will, from the beginning of 1913, be carried on at North Geelong, Victoria.

The Training Ship. — A vessel has been provided on which to instruct the large body of seamen and petty-officers required to **man the fleet**. Boys who pass the tests may enter upon the training at the age of 14½ years.

CHAPTER XI.

A SOLDIER'S TRAINING, AND WHAT IT DOES.

"Was there a man dismayed?

Not though the soldier knew
Someone had blundered."

—Tennyson.

XXV. DISCIPLINE.

1. IN some matters, British citizens who are in the Navy or Army are under different laws from those who belong to neither. It has been found that no army and no fleet can be well governed and directed unless there is strict **discipline** kept among all those in it. You know what discipline is, do you not? It is the habit of obedience to orders given by those who have the right to give them. It is the habit of acting according to rules laid down and practised beforehand, and of working together with others in such a way that there may be no confusion or dispute.

2. When boys and girls go out of school in order, one by one, class by class, they show that they have learnt the use of discipline. When they do their drill, moving their hands or their feet together at the word of command, they show that they have learnt the use of discipline.

3. There are very few things in the world which we should not do better for a little discipline, for **practice, patience, faith in others**, and **obedience to just orders**, which are the things that go to make

AN ENGLISH ARCHER.

up discipline, are useful in all that we have to do.

4. But in the Navy and Army, above all, it is necessary that discipline should be absolute and strict, not because the good qualities I have told you of are more necessary to a soldier or a sailor than they are to any other man, but because, in the dangers and difficulties of war, the consequences of being without any of them would be so terribly serious. I will give you some examples of the use of discipline in time of war.

Practice.

5. In the great war with France in the reign of Edward III., the English archers were over and over again victorious. And what was the reason? Simply that every boy as he grew up was made to fire at a mark with a long bow until he became a good archer. When the time of battle came, he won because he had had *practice*: the enemy were beaten because they had neglected to practise.

Patience.

6. To give you an example of the value of *patience* as a part of discipline, I cannot do better than tell you the story of how **Admiral Nelson** watched the French fleet. It was in the year 1805 when the

French, under **Napoleon Buonaparte**, having won a great many victories on land and having conquered nearly all other nations of Europe, were trying to invade and conquer England. The French fleet, at that time, was in the harbour of Toulon in the South of France, and it was most important that it should not be allowed to escape and join Buonaparte, who was waiting for it with his army just opposite Dover. For months and months, through all the storms of winter, Admiral Nelson lay in wait off the mouth of Toulon Harbour, watching the enemy as a cat watches a mouse.

7. It was a weary task, but Nelson was equal to it. As Southey, who wrote his life, truly says, "The patience with which he watched Toulon was an example of perseverance at sea which had never been surpassed." From May 1803 to August 1805, two years and three months in all, he went out of his ship but three times; each of these times was upon the King's service, and on no occasion did his absence exceed one hour. Encouraged by so good an example, the men on board the Admiral's ship were as determined and as patient as their commander, and at last the reward came. The French fleet escaped, it is true, but Nelson followed them. He chased them across the Atlantic to the West Indies and back.

8. When he returned to Portsmouth after his long pursuit, he feared after all that the enemy had escaped him, for he could get no news of them. But

ADMIRAL LORD NELSON.
*FROM THE PAINTING BY
SIR WM. BEECHEY, R.A.*

he was not long in starting off after them. He found them at last off the coast of Spain, and on the 21st October 1805, he fought the great battle of **Trafalgar**, in which he totally defeated the French and Spanish fleets, and took away the last fear of invasion. As you know, he lost his life in the moment of victory, but he has left behind him the lesson of how great is the need of patience as a part of discipline, and how great results may be won by patient waiting, no less than by courage and readiness in attack.

XXVI. FAITH IN OTHERS

1. When the battle of **Inkerman** in the Crimean War was fought, our troops were surrounded by a thick mist, and while they were thus shrouded in darkness, they were attacked by many thousands of the Russians. No man could see what his neighbours were doing; it was impossible to tell whether on the right side or the left the enemy had not got the victory; there was only one thing to be done, namely, for each man to do the best he could, trusting that every one of his comrades would do the same.

2. This is what our soldiers did. Their orders were to stop and fight, and each of them carried out his orders. They *had faith in others*, and in each other, and, in the end, the battle of Inkerman was won.

Obedience to Lawful Orders

3. Not very long ago, a British ship-of-war, the *Megæra*, was overtaken in a storm and greatly injured. The water began to pour into her, and it was plain that unless she could be run on shore, she must sink, and those on board lose their lives. There was only one way of running the ship on shore, and that was for the engineers and stokers to remain in the engine-room far below the water, and to keep the engines going full speed. It was probable, almost certain, that when the ship struck the shore, she would fall over on her side, and that none but those on deck would escape with their lives.

4. But the engineers and stokers had orders to keep the fires burning and the engines working, and, to obey their orders, they must stay below and run the risk of a terrible death. They did stay below, and at last the sinking ship was run full speed on to the shore.

5. Mercifully, she remained stuck fast, and not only those on deck, but the brave men down below were able to escape. But it was to their efforts that the whole crew owed their preservation; they had saved the ship *because they had obeyed orders*. You will see from these examples how great is the need for discipline in the Navy and Army.

The Value of Discipline

6. It is, indeed, so great that special rules and laws are made to punish those who disobey orders, who neglect their duty, and who are guilty of cowardice or misconduct in time of war.

7. These special rules are called "*Martial Law*," and though it seems hard at first that a man should be severely punished for doing that which, if he were not a soldier or a sailor, he would not be punished for at all, you will soon see that it is just, as well as necessary. For, suppose a soldier were to refuse to obey his sergeant because he thought that he knew better what ought to be done; then why should not the sergeant in his turn refuse to obey his captain, the captain his colonel, and so on? Plainly, at that rate, each man would be going his own way, and the enemy would have very little trouble in sending such a disorderly army to the right-about.

8. Or, again, suppose a soldier were to fall asleep at his post while he was keeping watch as a sentinel. Falling asleep is not wrong in itself, but think what may be the consequences. Over and over again, great armies have suffered defeat, ships have been taken, and thousands have lost their lives because those whose duty it was to watch against surprise neglected their charge. For the safety of all, therefore, it is right that the man who falls asleep at his post should be punished in the severest manner.

9. And, lastly, if a sailor or soldier proves himself a coward before the enemy, it is right that he should be punished at once and severely. For if a man is allowed to set the bad example of trying to save himself by giving way to his fears, then we may be sure that others will be moved by his bad example, or discouraged by his flight, and that a great advantage will be given to the enemy. So when we come to consider the consequences of these things, we shall understand why it is that it is right to punish under martial law.

10. But what is true for one man who is a soldier or a sailor is true for another. The sergeant will make the private soldier obey him, but if he wants him to do so, he must, in his turn, be ready to obey the captain, who gives him orders; and the captain, in his turn, must make his own wishes respected, but he must himself be a pattern of obedience to his superiors.

11. And so on, from rank to rank, from the highest to the lowest. There can be no shame in accepting orders from those who have themselves learnt to obey, and you may be sure that if ever you hear a sailor or soldier speak ill of discipline, and complain of having to obey orders, he is a black sheep; he will do very little credit to his ship or to his regiment.

The Loss of the "Birkenhead"

12. Before I finish this chapter, I will give you one more story which will show you how noble a thing discipline may become. It is another story of the sea, only this time the heroes of the tale are soldiers, not sailors.

13. A great ship, the *Birkenhead*, was sailing along the coast of Africa; on board of her were a number of soldiers, and besides the soldiers were many women and children. Suddenly the ship struck on a rock, and the water began to pour into her so fast that at last it became clear that, in spite of all the efforts of the crew, she must soon sink. No help was in sight, the only way of escape was by the boats,

THE WRECK OF THE "BIRKENHEAD".

but the boats were too few to carry the whole number of those who were now crowded on the deck of the unhappy ship. Who were to go? The strong men who could try to save themselves, or the weak women and weaker children who were at their mercy?

14. To the credit of the British Army, there was no hesitation. The officer commanding the soldiers gave them the order to fall in upon the deck, just as they had often done before in the barrack-yard. There in order they stood, while the sailors of the ship helped the women and children into the boats. Not a man broke from the ranks, not a man complained; the power of discipline was felt even in that terrible moment, and when at last the shattered ship sank into the dark waters, the red-coated English soldiers who went down with her had won a victory as glorious as any that has ever been won on the hardest-fought battlefield.

15. One thing remains for me to tell you about the loss of the *Birkenhead*. King William of Prussia, who afterwards became Emperor of Germany, heard the story. He thought, rightly, that no better lesson of the true value of discipline to a soldier could well be given. The story was translated into German, and by the order of the King was read aloud to the soldiers at the head of every regiment in the Prussian Army as an example of the value of discipline.

CHAPTER XII.
BRITAIN AND HER COLONIES

"Britain's myriad voices call,
Sons, be wedded each and all,
Into one imperial whole,
One with Britain, heart and soul!
One life, one flag, one fleet, one Throne!
Britons, hold your own!"

— Tennyson

"We learned from our wistful mothers
To call old England home."

— Kipling, The Native-Born

XXVII. THE PEOPLE OF GREATER BRITAIN

1. I MUST ask you to look once again at the map at the beginning of this book, and to count up once more the number of places marked, which, as I told you, are the places where the Union Jack flies, and where our fellow-countrymen live and work.

2. There is not a corner of the world where you will not see the red colour.

3. In **British Columbia** in the North; in our own **Australian continent**, and in **New Zealand** in the South; at **Hong Kong** and **Singapore** in the East; and in **Canada** and **Jamaica** in the West, you will find it; and when you see how far it spreads, and how great a part of the earth it covers, you may well ask, How can these colonies and

possessions, each and all, be preserved and protected from nations who would like to possess them and enjoy the wealth they yield?

4. The task would be too great for the United Kingdom, with all its strength, and with all its wealth. But fortunately its inhabitants are not left to do the work alone. Those who live far across the sea have not so changed from what their ancestors were at home that they are not ready and able to fight in their own defence and for their own rights.

5. Just as in Australia, so in Canada and New Zealand, there are men trained to the use of arms, and to the handling of ships of war; and there can be no doubt that, if any of these great colonies were to be attacked by a foreign nation, they would not be left to fight their battles alone, but, from every part of the Empire, help would speedily be sent to it.

6. Yes; only a few years ago, proof was given that those who had left Britain's shores and had gone to seek their fortunes in far-off colonies had not forgotten the country from which they sprang, and of whose greatness they are so proud. Not only had they not forgotten it, but they showed clearly to all the world that they must be counted with by any nation which seeks to injure the Old Country.

How the Colonies Helped the Old Country

7. In the year 1899, the Boers of the Transvaal declared war against Britain, and the Boers of the Orange Free State joined them. It was found necessary to send out a large army to South Africa to protect the Cape Colony and the Colony of Natal. It was at this time that the British people throughout the Empire showed that they were willing to help the Mother-country in time of need. Canada, Newfoundland, Australia, and New Zealand all sent their soldiers to fight side by side with those of Britain: 8,400 men came from Canada, 15,553 from the Australian continent, 6,513 from New Zealand, and 862 from little Tasmania.

8. Nor were other parts of the Empire behindhand. Volunteers came from India, from Ceylon, and from many other places, all ready to give their lives for the safety of the Empire.

9. Never before had so great a number of our countrymen from over the seas come forward to fight for the common cause. All these men served of their own free will, and with the permission, and in many cases the help, of the Government of the country from which they came.

10. It is not in the power of Britain to compel the Colonies to aid with their soldiers in time of war. But what happened in the case of South Africa has shown the nations that if ever Britain is in real danger, and is threatened by a powerful enemy, there will be thousands and tens of thousands of English-speaking men throughout the world who will be ready and willing to come forward and strike a blow for the safety and honour of the Old Country.

11. Nor must it be forgotten that the Colonies may be in as great danger as the United Kingdom itself. When such a danger arises, the armies and fleets of Britain will always be at hand to protect them. At present, the British Navy alone has to defend the whole of the British Empire and all its trade.

12. Australia and New Zealand (as you have read), the Cape Colony and Natal also, have made a beginning towards lightening this burden, and contribute yearly towards the cost of the Navy; and Australasian sailors now serve in the Royal Navy.

13. It will be seen, therefore, that the Navy and Army of Britain will not be without help in a great war. But the fact that the people of the British Empire are learning to act together for their common defence ought to make those who live in the United Kingdom, the centre and most important part of the Empire, very careful to avoid an unjust quarrel. They have not only themselves to consider, but also the millions of their fellow-countrymen in distant lands. And if this is the duty of those who live in the United Kingdom, it is

equally the duty of the people of Canada, Australia, New Zealand, and South Africa to remember that, if their quarrels are Britain's quarrels, they must take care that in these quarrels they shall always have justice on their side.

The Horrors of War

14. And before I finish these chapters upon our sailors and soldiers, whether they are those who belong to the regular Navy and Army, the Militia, or the Volunteers, I will say one thing which is true of all of them and of the work which they have to do.

15. The work of sailors and soldiers is to fight. And there are times when, as I have already told you, it is right and necessary that they should do so. But we must never forget for a moment that war, even though it be justly undertaken, is one of the most fearful misfortunes which can befall a people. Happily, we in Australia have had no experience of war within our borders.

16. We ought to be thankful that it is so; but we must remember that no war can ever be fought without causing pain, and sorrow, and ruin, and death to many, and that even worse than the outward misfortunes which war causes are the bad and cruel feelings—the hatred, the cruelty—which it often gives rise to in the hearts of those who make it or take part in it.

17. I trust that none of you will ever see a battlefield, or visit a country just after it has been swept by war. If you are ever tempted to think that war is a glorious thing, or that fighting can ever be anything but horrible, try to learn from the accounts of those who have seen real war what its results always are and must be.

18. Think of the dead and dying on the battlefield, the long trains of wounded, the hospitals with their scenes of agony, the ruined houses, the crops scattered, the fields uncultivated; and then, again, far from the scene of battle, the relations and friends of those who have been fighting, sorrowing over the dear ones they have lost; and

then, one step farther still, picture to yourselves the poverty that is caused by trade being stopped, and business being interfered with, and by the hard-earned money of the people being spent upon the Army, and you will begin to understand what are some of the consequences of war.

Unjust Wars

19. And, if all these things be true of a war which is necessary and just, how much more dreadful must be the consequences of entering upon *a war which is neither necessary nor just!* Then, to all the suffering and misery which I have described, would be added the shame and guilt of having brought upon tens of thousands of innocent persons the consequences of our own folly and our own bad passion.

20. England in the past has not always been free from the charge of entering upon wars for bad reasons, for insufficient reasons, or without enough thought of the consequences. There is no more important duty which you, all of you, whether boys or girls, will have to perform as British citizens when you grow up, than to keep your Country from entering upon unjust or unnecessary wars.

21. The decision between peace and war will rest with you, for nowadays we cannot say, as in the old times, that the Country is driven into war by kings, by the nobles, or by any small number of people. The whole people of the United Kingdom, at least, and, to some extent, of the self-governing portions of the Empire, now have a voice in determining whether there shall be war or not. And if the Imperial Government ever makes war unjustly, the blame of it will henceforward lie upon the shoulders of every citizen who has not done his or her best to prevent it.

CHAPTER XIII.
THE FLAG. – PART I.

"Here and here did England help me; how can I help England? Say."

— Browning.

"What is the flag of England? Winds of the world, declare!"

— Kipling.

XXVIII. THE UNION JACK.

1. I HOPE you all know the "**Union Jack**," the British flag; at any
rate, here is a picture of it, which will tell you what it is like. After
all, perhaps some of you will say, What is the use of giving us a lesson about the Union Jack; what can there be to tell about it that
we do not know?

2. We know that it is a pretty pattern, made of pieces of cloth
sewn together; we know that it is used for decorating the streets
when there are processions, and it is carried by soldiers and sailors
in battle. Now, all these things are true, but they are not the whole
truth, for there is, indeed, a great deal more to be said about the
Union Jack than this. In the first place, how do we come to have a
flag at all, and what is the meaning of it?

3. The flag is now the outward sign of the authority of the British
people. In itself, it is true, it is only a piece of silk or bunting;[22] but
really it is more than this, for it is known to all the world that it is the

22   Bunting, the material of which large flags are made.

THE CROSS OF
"ST. GEORGE"
FOR ENGLAND.

THE CROSS OF "ST.
ANDREW" FOR
SCOTLAND.

THE CROSS OF
"ST. PATRICK"
FOR IRELAND.

THE "UNION JACK."

sign which the British people have chosen to distinguish themselves
and their possessions all over the world, and to show to other nations
where Britain claims to govern and to be obeyed.

4. It is not, perhaps, very easy to understand what I have just
told you until you come to some examples which I will give you of
the use of the flag, and the purposes which it ought rightly to serve.
The UNION JACK is made up of the three Crosses of ENGLAND,
SCOTLAND, AND IRELAND, and is thus truly the Flag of the

Union. In the early history of England the Red Cross of St. George by itself was the Flag of England. When the Crowns of England and Scotland were united at the accession of James the VI. of Scotland to the throne of England, under the title of James the 1st, King of Great Britain and Ireland, the White Cross (or Saltire) of St. Andrew was added to the Cross of St. George; but it was not until the Act of Union between England and Scotland in 1707 that the flag containing the Crosses of England and Scotland became by law the National Flag. In 1801, after the Union with Ireland, the Red Cross of St. Patrick was added, and thus the UNION JACK was made up.

A LIST OF THE VARIOUS COUNTRIES, ISLANDS, TERRITORIES, AND POSSESSIONS WHICH MAKE UP THE "BRITISH EMPIRE" AND IN WHICH THE "UNION JACK" FLIES

(THE FIGURES GIVEN IN THIS LIST ARE THOSE OF THE LAST AVAILABLE STATISTICS.)

THE BRITISH ISLANDS

(1911 Census)

POPULATION:

England and Wales	36,075,269
Scotland	4,761,445
Ireland	4,381,951
The Isle of Man	52,034
The Channel Islands	96,000

Great Countries Chiefly Inhabited by Men of the British Race

NORTH AMERICA

Canada	7,185,000
Newfoundland	238,614

AUSTRALASIA

New South Wales	1,621,677
Victoria	1,307,304
Queensland	575,987
South Australia	408,146
Western Australia	294,203
Tasmania	188,049
New Zealand	1,046,543

Places Colonized by Men of British Race, but in which the Natives of British Descent are Outnumbered by Natives or Those of Some Other Race

SOUTH AFRICA

Union of South Africa	2,510,000
Cape of Good Hope	1,429,004
Natal	1,194,830
Transvaal	1,268,716
Orange Free State	528,174
Basutoland	409,016
Bechuanaland	127,000
Swaziland	83,600

(Note: In the South African Colonies there is a large number of persons of Dutch descent as well as the natives.)

WEST AFRICA

Gambia	14,000
Gold Coast	1,160,000
Sierra Leone	1,149,000
Nigeria	16,000,000

ASIA

Straits Settlements	836,661
Malay, Borneo, and Sarawak	305,097

SOUTH AMERICA

British Guiana	304,097
British Honduras	44,156

Islands Forming Part of the Empire and Colonized by Men of British Race, but in which there is still a Large Number of Natives or Persons not of British Race

Bahamas (West Indies)	61,077
Barbados (North Atlantic)	194,500
Jamaica (West Indies)	831,383
Fiji Islands (Pacific Ocean)	139,541
Ceylon (Indian Ocean)	4,106,350
Mauritius (Indian Ocean)	373,000
Labuan (China Seas)	40,000
Papua, or New Guinea (East Indies)	43,000
Trinidad and Tobago (West Indies)	351,318
Windward Islands (West Indies), including Grenada, St. Lucia, & St. Vincent	191,238

Places Retained Partly for Commercial Purposes, but Chiefly as Naval or Military Ports to Protect the Empire

MEDITERRANEAN

Gibraltar	18,581
Malta	216,879
Cyprus	257,527

RED SEA

Aden, Perim, and Socotra	55,074

CHINA SEAS

Hong Kong	450,000
Wei-hai-Wei	37,000

NORTH ATLANTIC

Bermuda	17,535

SOUTH ATLANTIC

Ascension	185
St. Helena	3,767

Possessions Under the Government of India, Occupied Chiefly by Natives, Though a Number of Men of British Race are There

India and Burma	294,317,092

Countries Under the Protection of the British Empire

Zanzibar and the parts of Africa striped in the map.

What the "Union Jack" Means.

5. But first, I think it will amuse you to know how it came about that the Union Jack became our national flag at all, and why it is that it is made up of the different patterns which you see in the picture. Let us take the pattern to pieces and put it together again. If you look carefully, you will see that the flag is made up of **a number of different crosses**, some red and some white. Now, each of these crosses has a meaning and a history.

6. First, there is a large red cross in the middle, which is shaped thus +, and which has a **white** border round it. That is called the **Cross of St. George**, and is the sign of England. If any of you is fortunate enough to have a new sovereign, he will see on it a picture of St. George killing the dragon, as is told in the old legend. From very early times St. George has been called the Patron Saint of England, and that is why the St. George's Cross is used upon the Union Jack to mark the place of England.

7. Then, if you look again, you will see that there is a white cross shaped like this X upon a blue ground. That, according to the old legend, is the **Cross of St. Andrew,** and was for long the sign of **Scotland**. And lastly, you will see that there is another cross of the same shape as the last, only red upon a white ground, and that is the **Cross of St. Patrick**, the great saint of **Ireland**; and so the three crosses have a meaning, and what they mean is **the union of England, Scotland, and Ireland.**

8. It was in the reign of George III., in the year 1801[23], that the idea of joining together the crosses of the three countries was first put into practice, to mark the union of those countries. Since that time, the Union Jack has been the national flag, and has been carried to every corner of the world.

23   The Union with Ireland was agreed to in 1800.

The Use of the Flag

9. Now that I have told you what the pattern on the Union Jack means, I must go back to what I said at the beginning of the chapter and explain to you what it is used for and what is the good of it.

10. You know that you often hear of flags carried by soldiers in battle, and by warships on the sea, but though the Union Jack has been carried by British soldiers and sailors in many a hard fight, you must not suppose that it has not any use in time of peace. Quite the contrary; indeed, some of the most useful purposes which our flag is made to serve have nothing whatever to do with wars and fighting.

11. In short, when the Union Jack is properly used in any place, it is as much as to say, *Here is something belonging to Britain, which the people of Britain have undertaken to protect.* It may be placed upon a fortress, or a ship of war, or it may be placed over the house in which a British Ambassador lives in a foreign country, while sometimes it is hoisted in a country which has never before had a civilised government, and then all the world knows that, from that time forward, Britain is going to undertake the government of that country, and is going to see that right and justice are done there.

12. When the flag is pulled down or taken away, then it is known that Britain has no longer the will or the power to have its wishes obeyed in the place from which the flag has gone.

XXIX. THE STORY OF KHARTOUM

1. In the year 1885, General Gordon was besieged within the walls of Khartoum by the Arabs. He had kept up a brave defence for a long time, and a relief party, under Sir Charles Wilson, was sent out to his assistance. The little band of soldiers and sailors had many difficulties to contend with. There were only two steamers, and they had to make their way through a country which was swarming

GENERAL GORDON.

with a determined enemy, who were already rejoicing over the successes they had gained.

2. But Sir Charles Wilson and his men still hoped that the brave general had been able to keep the British flag flying over the city. For hours the two steamers made their way up the river, and at last, with very great difficulty, they got near to the besieged city. The enemy fired at them from both banks, and many of the party were wounded, but still they pressed on with unabated courage, for they were determined to save their countryman if he were still alive.

3. Soon all eyes were strained to see if the flag were still waving over the house where Gordon had lived so long, and which he had defended so bravely. Alas, they looked in vain! *The flag was not there*, and then they knew that they were indeed too late, that the day was lost, and that Khartoum had fallen into the hands of the enemy. All this they learnt in a moment, when they saw the flag was no longer flying.

The Flag at Lucknow

4. Happily, we have not always been too late, and I will tell you another story of danger and rescue where the flag was still flying when the rescuers came.

5. It was at the famous siege of **Lucknow**, in India, during the terrible mutiny of the native soldiers against the British Government, of which I have already told you something.

6. The whole of the white inhabitants of the city—men, women,

and children—with a few faithful natives, were shut up in a large house called **the Residency**, and surrounded by thousands of the enemy. They were exposed by day and night for nearly five months to the bullets of the enemy. Many were killed, many wounded, and many fell sick under the terrible heat of the Indian sun.

7. **Sir Henry Lawrence**, the brave general in command, was killed by a cannon shot, but still the little band refused to give in. At one time, their hopes revived when **General Havelock**, with a small number of British soldiers, broke through the enemy and made his way into the Residency; but so great was the number of the besiegers that the rescuers found themselves shut up in their turn, and unable to get out. So passed three weary months, till hope died away and the end seemed near.

The Relief

8. But help was at hand. **Sir Colin Campbell**, with 5,000 fresh soldiers, was advancing by forced marches to the relief of the besieged city.

9. Over and over again, it seemed impossible that his little army could cut their way through the forces of the enemy, now elated by their victories. But one great thought was always in the minds of every one of the rescuers, from the general downwards—the lives of their countrymen, and, more than that, of their countrywomen and children, depended upon their success.

10. What would be the fate of their countrymen if they arrived too late? And so, under the scorching sun, and under the bullets of the enemy, they pressed on, and as at last they came near the city, the question rose to every man's lips—"Is it too late?"

11. Then, as the distant walls and towers of Lucknow came in sight, they turned their eyes upon the one building still surrounded by the smoke of battle, and there, above the Residency of Lucknow, they beheld **the Union Jack** still waving, and the flag told them

THE SECOND RELIEF OF LUCKNOW. 1857.

from afar off that they were not too late, that their work was not in vain, and that, ere another day was passed, they might press to their hearts the loved ones who so long had stood upon the brink of death.

12. There is a great poem by **Tennyson** which tells the story of the Siege of Lucknow, and of the first relief by Sir Henry Havelock. I hope you will read it for yourselves, but one or two verses I will give you now. First, the poet describes the besieged fortress with the Union Jack still floating over the shattered walls of the Residency, and gives us a picture of the sufferings and dangers of the little garrison:—

13. Banner of England! Not for a season, O banner of Britain,
      hast thou
Floated in conquering battle or flapt to the battle-cry!
Never with mightier glory than when we had reared thee on high,
Flying at top of the roof, in the ghastly siege of Lucknow,
Shot thro' the staff or the halyard,[24] but ever we raised thee anew,
And ever upon the topmost roof our banner of England blew.
Frail were the works that defended the hold that we held with our
      lives—
Women and children among us—God help them—our children
      and wives!
Hold it we might—and for fifteen days or for twenty at most.
"Never surrender, I charge you, but every man die at his post!"
Voice of the dead whom we loved—our Lawrence, the best of the
      brave,
Cold were his brows when we kissed him—we laid him that night
      in his grave.
"Every man die at his post!"—and there hailed on our homes and
      halls
Death from their rifle bullets, and death from their cannon balls;
Death in our innermost chamber, and death at our slight
      barricade;

24   Halyard, the rope for hauling up the flag on the staff.

Death while we stood with the musket, and death while we
    stooped to the spade;
Death to the dying, and wounds to the wounded—for often there
    fell,
Striking the hospital wall, crashing thro' it, their shot and their
    shell.

14. And the poem ends with the glad news of the relief, and the
meeting of General Havelock's soldiers with the poor women and
children whom they had come to rescue:—

Hark! cannonade, fusillade! Is it true what was told by the scout?
Outram and Havelock breaking their way through the fell
    mutineers?
Surely the pibroch[25] of Europe is ringing again in our ears!
All on a sudden the garrison utter a jubilant shout,
Havelock's glorious Highlanders answer with conquering cheers,
Sick from the hospital echo them, women and children come out,
Blessing the wholesome white faces of Havelock's good Fusileers,
Kissing the war-hardened hand of the Highlander wet with their
    tears;
Dance to the pibroch!—Saved! we are saved! Is it you? Is it you?
Saved by the valour of Havelock! Saved by the blessing of Heaven!
"Hold it for fifteen days?—We have held it for eighty-seven!"
And ever aloft on the palace roof the old banner of England flew.

15. I have told you these two stories of failure and success, to
show you how the flag plays the part of a sign and an emblem to the
world. At Khartoum, the flag was gone, and that meant that Britain
had no longer any power there, for good or for evil. At Lucknow,
the flag still floated, and from it men knew that the power of Britain
was still upheld.

16. As to the story of Khartoum, or the story of Lucknow, they

25   Pibroch, the war song of the Scotch Highlanders.

THE RELIEF OF LUCKNOW

are well worth reading in some books which tell you all about them at full length. They are splendid stories of bravery and endurance, which will make you all feel proud of your countrymen. I have told you about them quite shortly here, only to show you what I meant about the flag.

CHAPTER XIV.
THE FLAG.—PART II.

"A great empire and little minds go ill together."
— *Burke.*

XXX. PEACE.

1. BUT the **Union Jack** has its uses in time of peace as well as in time of war. Always remember that there is a great saying, which you will find repeated in your histories: "*No slave can breathe under the flag of England.*"

2. What is the meaning of this saying? It means that as, **by the law of the land, no man can be a slave**, so wherever the British flag waves, everyone is and must be free.

3. It may seem strange that I should think this so important, for you may well ask who could think of making slaves of other men nowadays?

4. Fortunately, this is true of all parts of the British Empire; but it was not always true, even of Britain and her colonies, and now, at this moment, there are still countries where the wicked practice of buying and selling men and women as slaves is still kept up.

The Flag and Slavery.

5. It is not much more than a hundred years ago, namely, in 1772, that the judges decided that, by the law of England, no man could be a slave within the British Islands; but though we were ashamed of slavery at home, we still allowed our countrymen to practise it abroad.

A MAN-OF-WAR CHASING A SLAVER.

6. At last, however, people in the United Kingdom began to understand how shameful it was that, in any part of the world, slavery should be allowed under the British flag, and, first of all, an effort was made by some of the best men in Parliament, the chief among whom was **Wilberforce**, to put an end to the **slave trade**; that is to say, the buying or capturing of slaves in Africa, and carrying them across the ocean to the colonies in America and the West Indian Islands. After many fruitless attempts, and much disappointment, the friends of the slave at last got their own way, and Parliament did away, once and for all, with the slave trade.

7. But to get rid of the slave trade was not enough. It was true that our flag no longer waved over those horrible slave ships; but in countries where the Union Jack showed that Britain bore rule, slaves were still kept, and bought and sold, and made to labour like dumb animals. The work of Wilberforce was not completed, but, fortunately, there were others no less zealous in the good cause than he, who gave up their lives to persuading their countrymen to do away with slavery everywhere throughout the world where British citizens had the making of the law.

8. One great difficulty had to be got over—the owners of the slaves had bought them under the law, and until the law was changed, they had a legal right to keep them. It was thought just, therefore, to give to the slave-holders some payment in money, so that they might not all be ruined by the change in the law. At last, the people and the Parliament were persuaded, and, in the year 1833, an Act of Parliament was passed by which all the slaves throughout the British Empire were set free, and a payment of twenty million pounds was made to the former slave-owners.

9. Now, at last, the country had its hands free, and could help others to get rid of the evil also.

10. All civilised nations have long agreed to put down the slave trade, and, whenever a slave trader sees the British flag on a ship of

war, he tries to escape, for he knows that the captain of the British ship has orders to take every slave ship that he sees, to set free the slaves, and to give up the trader to be punished.

Freedom under the Union Jack.

11. Not very long ago, some slaves on the African coast swam off to a British ship and claimed to be free under the Union Jack. By some mistake, they were sent back to their masters; but when this was known at home, everyone was angry and indignant, and orders were given that such a thing should never be allowed to happen again. So now, whenever a slave can place himself under the shadow of the Union Jack, he knows that he will be free, and that no man will be allowed to claim him.

12. Then again, as I told you, the flag is used to show that some uninhabited or uncivilised country has been taken in the name of our King, and that, from that time, it is to become part of the British Empire. Look at the island on your map called **New Guinea**. There you will see a patch coloured red, which, as I told you, means that it is part of the British Empire.

A few years ago, that red patch would not have been there, for it was only in the year 1883 that a party of our countrymen landed on the island and hoisted the Union Jack in the name of Queen Victoria. The picture shows the Union Jack being hauled up to the top of the flag staff while the sailors and soldiers fire a salute.

The Flag of Australia.

13. The mention of the annexation of New Guinea brings your thoughts near home, and, perhaps, you are now thinking of the flag we have been permitted to fly as specially our own—the flag of the Commonwealth of Australia.

14. The design of this flag, which was chosen out of about 30,000 shown at a flag exhibition held in Melbourne, is very appropriate, as

HOISTING THE BRITISH FLAG IN NEW GUINEA (FIRING THE FEU DE JOIE).

it symbolises much that we prize highly. The first quarter is filled with the Union Jack, which signifies that Australia is a part of the British Empire, and that its people share in the glories of the British race; on the second and fourth quarters is displayed the five stars of the Southern Cross—the most beautiful constellation in the Southern skies; and the third quarter is occupied by a large six-pointed[26] star, which typifies the union in interests and aims of the six States of the Commonwealth.

Why We Should Honour the Flag.

15. I have told you enough to show you what the flag is, and what is the use of it. I want you to remember it is nothing in itself; but because it stands before other people as the mark of our country, it means a great deal. It is right and useful that men should honour and love the flag, and be prepared to lose their lives in defending it, as many of our countrymen have done before now; but we must bear in mind that it is not really the piece of coloured silk that is worth dying for, but only the honour and reputation of the country which has chosen it for its own.

16. And so long as you do your best to make the British Empire the first among the nations in all that is right and just, so long will you do well to honour and to love the Union Jack, which, by the bravery and the wisdom of our forefathers, has become so famous.

Empire Day.

17. This talk about the flag will bring into the minds of my readers some thoughts **of Empire Day**, as on it, no doubt, they go through the ceremony of saluting the Union Jack. Why should we celebrate that day?

26   Afterwards, when Papua (British New Guinea) was brought under the administration of the Commonwealth Parliament, another point was added to the star.

THE FLAG OF THE COMMONWEALTH OF AUSTRALIA.

18. During the long reign of Queen Victoria, her birthday was kept up; and after her death, in 1901, the idea occurred to some that **the 24th of May**—so long a holiday—should continue to be set aside for patriotic observances, by which means the memory of the good Queen would be preserved, and the patriotism of the British people deepened. The idea gained wide acceptance, and by 1905 the movement had spread throughout the Empire. Let us all take our part in supporting it vigorously.

19. The Earl of Meath, who was foremost in securing the establishment of **Empire Day**, thus expresses the objects of its advocates:— "We wish to instil into the rising generation a becoming desire to devote themselves heart and soul to the good of their fellow-creatures, and especially of their fellow subjects within the Empire. We wish them to realise that the duties and responsibilities attaching to British citizenship are many and grave, and that it behoves each individual to prepare him or herself for the due performance of these duties. We need to learn the meaning of the terms, loyalty, patriotism, respect, obedience, self-sacrifice."

CHAPTER XV.
TAXATION.

"All for each and each for all."

XXXI. WHAT ARE TAXES?

1. IN the last few chapters, I have been telling you about all the different things that have to be done in order that the country may be well governed and protected. You have learnt how justice is done, how the Post Offices, the Treasuries, the Education Departments, and the various other Departments are worked.

2. Of course, it is quite plain that all these things cannot be done for nothing. The judges must be paid, the postmen, the Treasury officials, the teachers, and the rest of the public officers must receive their salaries, and money must be provided for all the different purposes which I have described to you. **How is this money to be got, who is to pay it, and how is it to be collected?** Let us first consider for whose good the money is spent, and then we shall soon see who ought to pay it.

3. Formerly, a great part of what is now the country of Holland lay beneath the sea. Year by year, for many centuries, the Dutch have laboured to reclaim from the waves the land on which their towns are built, and the fields upon which they feed their cattle and grow their corn. To keep out the waters of the German Ocean, great embankments of earth and masonry, called **dykes**, have been built for miles along the coast. Outside the dykes is the sea. Inside, and below the level of the sea, are the fertile fields of Holland.

4. If once the dykes were to break, the water would come pouring in, and would destroy in a few hours the work of many years' patient labour. If such a calamity were to happen, it is not the rich only or the poor only, it is not the farmer alone nor the manufacturer, but everybody, rich and poor, high and low, who would be overwhelmed

by the rush of the waters. It is, therefore, necessary, for the protection of all, that the dykes should be kept up and in good repair. And as everybody alike is protected by the dykes, so everyone is called upon to pay for maintaining them.

What is maintained for the public good should be paid for out of the public money.

5. Some time ago, a very large building, known as the "**Law Courts**," was built in Melbourne. Inside it are the Courts in which judges sit to try cases which are brought before them from all parts of Victoria. And, besides the Courts, there are a very large number of offices where those who are entrusted with the duty of administering justice and looking after the proper carrying out of the law do their work. This great building cost no less than £350,000, a very large sum, as you will allow, and far more than any single person could afford to pay.

Who Pays?

6. Now, who did pay this large sum? It is plain that if only those persons who used the Courts—those who went to law to get their own disputes settled by the judges—had to pay, they would very soon be ruined; and, indeed, they would never try to get justice done to them if it cost so dear. How, then, has the money been got? First of all, we must consider who it is that uses the Courts, and who it is that goes to law. As a matter of fact, the number of people who really do go to law is not very large. But, though everyone does not use the Courts, everyone has the right to use them whenever he requires to do so.

7. The law exists for the benefit of all, rich and poor alike, and it is not only those who actually have their disputes settled before the judges who get the benefit of the law. As long as there are judges who will decide fairly, and Courts in which every man can get justice done to him, so long is the country safe from all the danger and

discontent which always spring up where there is no true justice. And thus it is, that though everybody does not use the Courts of Justice, yet everybody benefits by them.

8. And so we come back to the question, Who ought to pay for building the Courts? and the answer is, Those who get the benefit of them ought to pay for them. But, as we have seen, everybody gets the benefit of them, and, *therefore, everybody ought to pay for them.* And this is what really happens—public works are paid for out of public money, generally money that has been borrowed for a certain number of years by the Government, to the repayment of which everyone contributes.

9. From these two illustrations, I hope you will understand what I am going to tell you about taxes and taxation, and that you will learn how it is that the money is collected, not only for building the Law Courts, but for doing all the great public works of which I told you in the last few chapters.

What Taxes Are.

10. Taxes are *payments made by all for the good of all.* There are many things which must be done in a great country like this which cannot possibly be done by separate people, but which must be undertaken by the Government of the country, for the benefit of all.

11. Thus, for instance, it is necessary, as I told you, that the **judges** should be paid, that the Courts of Law should be built, that the **postmen** should receive their wages, that our **soldiers** and **sailors** should get their pay, and that **forts** to guard our ports should be built. All these things are necessary for everybody alike. It is true that everybody does not go to law, but it is true, too, that if there were no judges, there would be no way of justly settling disputes, and no way of punishing wrongdoers, and we should find out very soon that a country in which there was neither law nor justice was one in which no man could live with safety and happiness.

12. So, too, with our soldiers and sailors. Everyone does not wish to go into the Army or Navy; very few people, it is to be hoped, wish the country to go to war for the sake of fighting only, but all of us, whatever our station in life, are made more secure because of the protection which the Army and Navy give to this country. And if you think for yourself, you will find many other things which are done for the good of all, and which, therefore, ought to be paid for by all.

13. The money to pay for these things comes from the *taxes*. I will tell you a little farther on what the taxes are and how they are collected.

You will see that all the objects which I have spoken about concern everybody in the country, wherever they may live and whatever may be their occupation.

Rates.

14. You know, from your own observation and from what you have read in a former chapter under "Local Government," that a great many things have to be done in every city and township for the comfort and convenience of those who live in them. Streets and roads, for instance, have to be made and repaired, drains dug and kept in order, and refuse got rid of. Of course, each man in the place could not give up enough of his time to keep in good condition the streets through which he passed, nor would it be convenient for him to dig a part of the drains, nor to carry to a distance and destroy the rubbish that accumulated about his house. So, for all these things and many others, it is usual to follow somewhat the same course that I told you was followed in the case of the judges, the postmen, and the soldiers. The citizens or townsmen join together to pay for these things which are necessary to all who live in the city or town. The payments which are made for these purposes are called *Rates*.

15. Of course, there is often a great difference between the things which are required in a large town and in a small township. In a large

town, for instance, the danger of fire is much greater than it is in a township, where most of the houses are apart from one another; and it is necessary, therefore, to provide fire engines and firemen in the one case, which are not needed in the other.

16. And even between two large towns there are very great differences, arising mainly from their position and the nature of the industries carried on in them.

17. For this reason, the collection of rates, unlike that of taxes, is left to the people of each city, borough, municipal district, shire, or other area, and is not decided by Parliament. An estimate of the amount of money required for the year is made, and the local governing body—usually called a **Council**—in order to raise it, strikes a rate on the value of the property within its control. Every owner of property has to pay so much—a shilling, one and three-pence, or whatever the Council has decided—in the pound on its annual value. To obtain the money, collectors are appointed, who send out notices to each occupier or owner of property, and if the amount claimed is not forwarded within a stated time, they call for it. The law is strict in enforcing the payment of rates.

18. The rates serve many purposes. They may pay for public baths, for the lighting of the streets, and the supply of water, as well as for those things we read of earlier in this chapter.

19. In addition to the Councils, there are, in the various States, **Trusts** and **Boards** to whom certain duties have been handed over by the Governments, and some of these are empowered to levy rates. For instance, we have Harbour Trusts to watch over and provide for the needs of shipping in certain ports, and Fire Brigade Boards to cope with the outbreaks of fire in cities and large towns. In some places, gas or electricity is supplied by private companies, who provide it at their own expense, and sell it to those who require it. It is true that the payments are sometimes called *Rates*, but they are not "rates" in the sense of the other payments.

XXXII. WHAT THE COUNTRY PAYS.

1. I will now give you one or two facts which will interest you about the quantity of money that is required in a single year for doing the work of the country.

2. You know how in every home so much money comes in and so much goes out. All the money that the father of the family or any other member of it earns, the profit made upon business or trade, and any other sums which are paid to those who live in the home, are incomings or income.

3. Everything that has to be paid away, such as rent, money for butchers' and grocers' bills, money for clothes, boots, and so on, make the outgoings or expenditure. If it is a wisely ordered household, care will always be taken that the **incomings** are more than the **outgoings**; and if it turns out that more has been spent than has been received, a wise man will at once set to work to see if he cannot give up some of the things that cost money, and do with a little less, so that at the end of the year he may have a little to the good, and have something to put into the bank instead of owing money to others.

4. So it is, or so it ought to be, with the country. On the one side there are the **incomings**, and on the other the **outgoings**; and it is always the duty of a good Government and a wise Parliament to spend less than is received.

The Country's Accounts.

5. For example, in a single year ended June, 1904, the incomings or **revenue** of the Australian States amounted to about thirty-three million two hundred thousand pounds, and the outgoings or **expenditure** to a slightly greater amount, exclusive of the expenditure of loan money on public works of a permanent kind.

6. Out of the thirty-three million and odd pounds spent, the officers who collected the customs and excise duties received, as remuneration, about £265,000; the post and telegraph officials,

£2,700,000; and the soldiers and sailors, £836,000. In paying the judges and police, and keeping up the gaols, nearly £2,000,000 went; two millions and a quarter were spent on education, and one and a third millions on asylums, hospitals, and other charitable institutions. It took no less than £8,355,337 to pay the interest on the public debt of the States. On water supply, over a million and a half were spent; and the working expenses of our railways and State tramways amounted to over seven millions and a half. There were many other items of expenditure, but I dare say that I have mentioned enough to cause you to exclaim in astonishment: "How is all this enormous amount of money to be collected, and who is to pay it?" To this I answer, "It is paid by the taxpayers, and is collected in two different ways."

Direct and Indirect Taxes.

7. There are what are called *direct* and *indirect* taxes. This seems at first rather a hard sentence to understand, but it is not so really; let me explain.

Direct Taxes.

8. **Direct taxes** are sums of money paid directly to the collectors appointed by the Government to take them. For instance, there is, in several of the States, a tax called the **income tax**, which every man who is in receipt of an income of more than a certain amount a year has to pay. No two States impose the same conditions for its payment, but if we examine those in force in South Australia, it will be sufficient. On all incomes derived from personal exertion, the people there[27] have to pay 4½d. in the £ up to £800, and 7d. over that amount; and on incomes obtained from property, 9d. in the £ up to £800, and 1s. 1½d. over that amount. Those whose incomes

27   This was so in 1904. Parliament may make changes annually in the Act. —*J. A. Sears, Melbourne.*

CUSTOM HOUSE, MELBOURNE.

are not more than £135 escape the tax, and on incomes less than £400, the tax is exacted only on the difference between £135 and the amount. Thus, a man with an income of £375 would have to pay annually to the Government 240 times 4½d., or £4 10s.

9. In most of the States there is **a tax**—so much in the £—levied by the Government on the **unimproved value of land**. Then again, there are many kinds of **licences**—a man who wishes to dig for gold must obtain a miner's right, a hawker must possess a licence to sell his goods, and so on.

10. These examples are given to show you what is the meaning of direct taxation.

Indirect Taxes.

11. Now, I must say a word to you about *indirect* taxation, and what that means. I dare say a good many of you have paid indirect taxes yourselves without knowing it. Indeed, the greater part of our revenue is derived from indirect taxes.

12. Every time you drink a **cup of coffee,** you are paying an *indirect tax*. Every time a man **smokes a pipe**, he is paying an indirect tax.

13. This seems rather strange at first sight, but it is quite true, as you will see when I have explained what I mean. As you know, all the coffee that is drunk in this country comes to us from abroad. The coffee which you buy at the grocers' shops has been grown in Ceylon, Arabia, Brazil, or some other hot country, and brought thence across the sea in ships.

14. As soon as the coffee reaches this country, the merchant who brings it has to declare how much there is in each cargo, and for every pound that is landed, he has to pay a tax, or customs duty, of several pence to the Government. In the year 1904, £26,619 was received in the way of taxes upon coffee.[28]

---

28   The amount of coffee imported was 1,880,216 lbs.; of tea there was very much more, namely, 27,270,206 lbs. There is no tax on tea.

15. But coffee is not the only thing which is taxed in this manner. **Wine, beer, spirits, sugar**, and hundreds of other articles are made to furnish part of the money which is required for the service of the country. On many of these articles, however, a customs duty has been placed, not for the purpose of raising revenue, but with the intention of encouraging their production or manufacture in Australia.

16. The taxes upon stimulants, such as beer, wine, and spirits, are very large, and this is quite right; for, in the first place, it is always best to tax those things which are only used for enjoyment or pleasure, and which are not really necessary for the use of man; and, in the second place, so much harm is done by the wrong use of beer, wine, and spirits, and drunkenness is so dreadful and horrible a thing, that, if anything at all is to be taxed, it is surely right that the strong drinks which are often the cause of so much misery should be chosen. During the twelve months which ended June, 1904 (the financial year 1903–4), taxes on stimulants yielded an amount not far short of £3,000,000.

17. Besides wine, beer, and spirits, there is another thing which is used by a great many people, but which is not really necessary to enable them to live, and that is **tobacco**; and tobacco, therefore, is heavily taxed too, the revenue derived from it in a year amounting to about £1,000,000. Taxes on things we **consume** are **indirect**.

XXXIII. PARLIAMENT VOTES THE TAXES.

1. There is one more thing to be remembered about them, and it is this—that, nowadays, it is those who pay the taxes who decide what they are to be, and how they are to be collected. This was not always so. There was a time when the King of England was accustomed to make the people pay whatever sums he chose. It was not long, however, before the injustice of this plan was felt; and as far back as the reign of King Henry III., the Parliament claimed the

right, which it has never since given up, of deciding how much the people should pay.

2. Of course, it is not the same thing to claim a right and to get others to recognise it. For many hundred years after the reign of Henry III., there were attempts made by kings to levy taxes without consulting Parliament; and very often Parliament was unable to prevent this being done.

3. One of the chief differences which brought about the Civil War in Charles I.'s time was a dispute as to the payment of a tax called Ship-money, which the King wished to collect illegally. He was resisted in his attempt by a very famous member of the House of Commons, **John Hampden** by name. The King's tax collectors came to John Hampden with a writ or order from the King's Court to compel him to pay, but Hampden refused, and said that he would not pay unless the judges declared that the King had a right by law to make the people pay the tax. And though at first Hampden seemed likely to suffer for his boldness, in the end the cause for which he gave his life was victorious; and now, in our day, there is no longer any dispute as to the right of Parliament, and Parliament alone, to vote taxes.

CHAPTER XVI.
OUR DUTY TOWARDS FOREIGN COUNTRIES.—PART I.

"Do unto others as you would they should do unto you."

XXXIV. THE "BARBARIANS."

1. THE ancient Greeks had a strange way of speaking of all foreigners, no matter who they were, as "**Barbarians**." It was the same whether they spoke of the educated and civilised people of Egypt, of the luxurious and warlike Persians, or of the wild Scythian tribes who passed their lives in a half-savage state in the country north of the Black Sea. To the Greek, they were alike one and all—Egyptian, Persian, Scythian; they were uncouth, outlandish, barbarian—in a word, not Greek.

2. In the same way, at the present time, the Chinese also speak of all foreigners—English, Americans, French, Germans—without any distinction, as "**Barbarians**." China to the Chinese is the only country in the world. If there are any other countries in the world, they are unimportant and uncivilised, and the people who live in them are only "**Barbarians**."

Look at Home.

3. It is easy to laugh at the Greeks of old, and at the Chinese of the present day, and to wonder at any people being so foolish as to think that no nation but their own deserves to be called civilised. But, after all, it is not quite certain that, if we were to look carefully, we

JOHN HAMPDEN REFUSING TO PAY SHIP-MONEY.

might not find something of the same kind nearer home. Australia is so shut off from the rest of the world by being an island that very many of the native-born never see foreign countries at all, and very seldom see the people who live in them. Some of us, perhaps, know a Frenchman, or a German, or an Italian, but we know very little indeed of the countries from which they come, and when we speak of them as foreigners, we often talk as if they were something quite different from ourselves.

4. Sometimes you will hear people, both grown-up men and women as well as children, talk scornfully of foreigners as if they thought them in some way inferior to themselves. And others you will hear talking as if all foreigners were their enemies, and as if it were the most natural thing in the world for the British and French, or the British and Germans, to be always quarrelling, always hating each other, always trying to take advantage of each other.

5. Whenever you hear anybody talking in this way, or whenever you feel inclined yourselves to talk or to think in such a fashion, it will be time for you to remember the Greeks and the Chinese, and to ask yourselves whether it was quite fair to laugh at them for holding such foolish opinions about their neighbours.

The Result of Ignorance.

6. After all, it is really just the same reason that made the Greeks of old, and the Chinese of to-day, talk of "Barbarians," that makes people in this country say harsh and unjust things about Germans, French, or Italians, and makes them hate or despise people of whom they really know nothing. The reason in both cases is **ignorance**.

7. A boy who lives till he is twenty in a little country town, and never goes out of it, will, perhaps, think that there is no building in the world so big as the Shire Hall, and no river so broad as the creek which runs through the town. But directly he leaves his home and travels abroad, he begins to find out that there are a great many things

in the world which he has not seen, and a good many, too, which he has never even heard of; and, before very long, he will stop talking about the wonders of his own home, unless he wants to be laughed at by the people whom he meets.

How Travel Teaches Us.

8. And so, in the same way, it is easy enough for us, as long as we live in this country, to persuade ourselves that there is very little that is good, or well done, or well arranged, outside it. But directly we cross the sea, we shall find out that there are, besides Australia, other great countries, each with its own beauties and its own advantages; excelling us in some points, inferior to us in others.

9. In each country in turn, we shall find men, women, and children living useful and happy lives such as we are accustomed to at home; and though we shall notice at first a great many differences in the manners and customs of those whom we see, the more we know of the people and their ways, the less real difference shall we find between them and ourselves.

10. Wherever we go, we shall find men and women working hard and honestly for their daily bread; we shall find children going to school, young men and women falling in love and marrying, men and women of all ages doing good in a hundred different ways which are not the less useful because they are not quite the ways we are accustomed to.

11. The first time we see a foreigner and hear him talk, we are sure to be struck by his strangeness and by the difficulty of understanding him; and the first time we set foot in a foreign country, we are sure to notice directly all the things which are unlike what we have been accustomed to at home. But if we get to know the foreigner better, or if we spend a longer time in the foreign country, we are nearly certain to find out that neither the one nor the other is really half so strange as we first thought.

An Example.

12. There is a story which teaches us a very good lesson about not laughing at things just because they seem strange, or despising other people because their manners and customs appear at first sight to be different from ours. As often as not, you will find out that the strange thing which you are laughing at is really to be found quite near home, only that we call it by a different name and use it in another fashion. I will tell you the story in the next chapter.

CHAPTER XVII.
OUR DUTY TOWARDS FOREIGN COUNTRIES — PART II.

"There are folk beyond the mountains." — German Proverb.

XXXV. A STRANGE COUNTRY

1. ONCE upon a time, a certain man was asked to give an account of his travels. "I will tell you," said he, "what I saw in a remarkable country which I lately visited, and in which I found a curious people whose manners and customs were as strange as they were ridiculous.

2. "The country in question was **an island**, and I believe I am not the only person who has visited it; and those others who have succeeded in reaching its shores will, I am certain, confirm the truth of my story, and convince you that what I say of this particular tribe is no collection of travellers' tales, but a true account of a real people who are not without some understanding and certain traces of civilisation.

An Account of the Tribe[29]

3. "I was once, about this time of the year, in a country where it was very cold, and the poor inhabitants had much ado to keep themselves from starving. They were clad partly in the skins of beasts made soft and smooth by a particular art, but chiefly in garments

---

29   The greater portion of this chapter is taken from Mrs. Barbauld's charming work, "Evenings at Home."

made from the outer covering of a middle-sized quadruped, which they were so cruel as to strip off his back while he was alive.

4. "They dwelt in habitations, part of which was sunk underground. The materials were either stones or earth hardened by fire; and so violent in that country were the storms of wind and rain, that many of them covered their roofs all over with stones. The walls of their houses had holes to let in the light; but to prevent the cold air and wet from coming in, they were covered with a sort of transparent stone, made artificially of melted sand or flints.

Their Diet

5. "Their diet, too, was remarkable. Some of them ate fish that had been hung up in the smoke till they were quite dry and hard; and, along with it, they ate either the roots of plants or a sort of coarse black cake made of powdered seeds. These were the poorer class; the richer had a whiter kind of cake, which they were fond of daubing over with a greasy matter that was the product of a large animal among them. This grease they used, too, in almost all their dishes; and, when fresh, it really was not unpalatable.

6. "They likewise devoured the flesh of many birds and beasts when they could get it, and ate the leaves and other parts of a variety of vegetables growing in the country — some absolutely raw, others variously prepared by the aid of fire. Another great article of food was the curd of milk, pulped into a hard mass and salted.

Their Drink

7. "For drink, they made great use of the water in which certain dry leaves are steeped. These leaves, I was told, came from a great distance. They had likewise a method of preparing a liquor of the seeds of a grass-like plant steeped in water, with the addition of a bitter herb, and then set to work or ferment. I was prevailed upon to taste it, and thought it at first nauseous enough, but in time I liked

it pretty well. When a large quantity of the ingredients is used, it becomes perfectly intoxicating.

8. "But what astonished me most was their use of a liquor so excessively hot and pungent that it seemed like liquid fire. I once got a mouthful of it by mistake, taking it for water, which it resembles in appearance; but I thought it would instantly have taken away my breath. Indeed, people are not unfrequently killed by it; and yet many of them will swallow it greedily whenever they can get it. This,

too, is said to be prepared from the seeds above mentioned, which are innocent and even salutary in their natural state, though made to yield such a pernicious juice.

Their Strange Birds and Plants

9. "I was glad enough to leave this cold climate; and about half a year after, I fell in with a people enjoying a delicious temperature of air, and a country full of beauty and verdure. The trees and shrubs were furnished with a great variety of fruits, which, with other vegetable products, constituted a large part of the food of the inhabitants. I particularly relished certain berries growing in bunches, some white and some red, of a very pleasant sourish taste, and so transparent that we might see the seeds at their very centre.

10. "Here were whole fields full of extremely odoriferous flowers, which, they told me, were succeeded by pods bearing seeds that afforded good nourishment to man and beast. A great variety of birds enlivened the groves and woods; among which I was entertained with one that, without any teaching, spoke almost as plainly as a parrot, though indeed it was all the repetition of a single word.

Their Manners

11. "The people were tolerably gentle and civilised, and possessed many of the arts of life. Their dress was very various. Many were clad only in a thin cloth made of the long fibres of the stalk of a plant cultivated for the purpose, which they prepared by soaking in water and then beating with large mallets.

Their Clothes

12. "Others wore cloth woven from a sort of vegetable wool growing in pods upon bushes. But the most singular material was a fine glossy stuff, used chiefly by the richer classes, which, as I was credibly informed, is manufactured out of the webs of caterpillars —

a most wonderful circumstance if we consider the immense number of caterpillars necessary to the production of so large a quantity of the stuff as I saw used.

13. "This people were very fantastic in their dress, especially the women, whose apparel consists of a great number of articles impossible to be described, and strangely disguising the natural form of the body. In some instances they seem to be very cleanly, but in others the Hottentots can scarce go beyond them — particularly in the management of their hair, which is all stiffened with the fat of swine and other animals, mixed up with powders of various colours and ingredients.

Their Odd Habits

14. "Like most Indian nations, they use feathers in the head-dress. One thing surprised me much, which was, that they bring up in their houses an animal of the tiger kind, with formidable teeth and claws, which, notwithstanding its natural ferocity, is played with and caressed by the most timid and delicate of their women. The language of this nation seems very harsh and unintelligible to a foreigner, yet they converse among one another with great ease and quickness."

What is the Name of the Country?

15. You do not want me to go any farther with this story. You have found me out already, I am sure; and you know that the strange country about which the traveller told his tale was none other than **England**, and that all the odd things that he described were only what people there, and indeed we in Australia, are quite accustomed to.

16. You know that the grease used in the dishes of the islanders is neither more nor less than butter, and that the large animal which produces it is the cow. The dried leaves which are soaked in water are tea-leaves; and, if you use your wits, you will easily find out that all the other things that are mentioned are, after all, old friends with new faces, and only seem odd because they are described in a way you are not accustomed to.

CHAPTER XVIII.
OUR DUTY TOWARDS FOREIGN COUNTRIES — PART III.

"Hatred is the child of ignorance and the father of strife."

XXXVI. A LESSON

1. WHAT I want you to learn from the story in the last chapter is not to judge foreigners and the countries from which they come too hastily. I want you to learn that it is foolish as well as wicked to say that all the people in another country are bad, or stupid, or ridiculous, because they think or do something of which you do not approve. It is foolish, because it generally happens that, if we were a little wiser, we should see that those whom we laugh at have a very good reason for doing what they do.

2. Judging too hastily about the actions of foreign peoples often leads to quarrels between nations; and such quarrels, as you know, often end in war — the most terrible misfortune which can overtake a country.

3. You will be astonished when you read history to find how small are the matters about which great quarrels have arisen and great wars have been fought.

The Story of the Two Knights

4. I dare say you know the story of the knights and the shield: how, in the olden time, two knights, riding to meet each other from different directions, saw hanging over their path a shield. "What a

beautiful golden shield," said the one. "Golden!" replied the other; "silver, you mean." "The shield is golden, and it is golden that I mean," said the first knight. "You must surely be a little weak of sight," says number two, "not to be able to tell gold from silver."

5. And so, the story runs, a pretty quarrel began, and only ended by the knights settling their difference in the knightly fashion of their day — by having a battle there and then to prove that their respective opinions were right; though how they could prove much by running each other through the body is not very plain.

6. At last, as they both lay bleeding and exhausted upon the ground, there came by a friar. To him, as he stanched their wounds, they explained the cause of their quarrel, and asked him, as a fair-minded person, to decide which of them was really in the right, for, inasmuch as neither of them had won the battle, neither could say that his view was the correct one.

7. "Tell us, holy father," they said, "is the shield gold or silver?" "Poor deluded men," replied the friar; "is this the cause of your quarrel? How easily you could have solved it with a little patience! Neither of you is right, neither of you wrong. Look at this shield; **one side is gold, and the other silver**. If you had only tried to look at the question from both sides, you would not be lying in this sorry plight."

The Moral

8. The moral of this story is plain enough. The two knights fought not in order to find out whether the shield were gold or silver — for it did not matter the least to either of them what it was made of — but they fought to satisfy their own pride, and because both of them thought it was finer to fight about a difference of opinion than to find out in a reasonable way what the truth was, and whether, when they knew the truth, it mattered the least bit in the world to either of them on which side it lay.

XXXVII. HOW WARS ARE BEGUN

1. It is wonderful how often the great countries of the world have followed the example of the two knights, and have quarrelled about the very smallest matters, and have entered upon great and terrible wars simply because their pride was wounded, and because they would not try to look at both sides of a question. When we consider how horrible a thing war is, and how great is the suffering which it inflicts not only upon those who fight, but upon all those to whom it brings sorrow, poverty, and pain at home, it becomes plain that anyone who helps to bring about a war is a very bad citizen and a very false friend of his country.

2. And yet there are always to be found men who are ready, when any little difference arises between two countries, to try to make their countrymen follow the example of the two knights. They will only look at their side of the shield, and will never stop to think that somebody with eyes as good as theirs sees something quite different on the other side.

3. And when they have once started the foolish quarrel, they do all they can, by saying bitter and unjust things of their opponents, to make it impossible for either side to look at the matter coolly — to take down the shield, and turn it over, and settle in a reasonable way whether there is anything worth fighting about at all.

Enemies of Their Country

4. Such men as these are **enemies of their country**, and we should all take the greatest pains not to be found among their number.

5. The safest way to do this, and the best way to do good service to the country, is for everyone — man or woman, boy or girl — to be even more careful in what they say about foreigners and foreign countries than about what they say of their own countrymen and their own country. At the same time, it is a special duty devolving upon every Australian to form for himself or herself an opinion as

THE KNIGHTS AND THE SHIELD.

to the amount of freedom that should be allowed to foreigners —
especially Asiatics — to settle in this country.

Some Good Rules to Remember

6. Always be civil and courteous to a foreigner; in the first place,
because it is your duty to be civil and courteous to everybody, and
especially to those who are strangers and far from their own friends.

7. In the second place, because as you behave to them so will they
judge of you; and when they return to their own country, they will
help to win friends or enemies for Britain, according as they have
found those English-speaking men and women whom they have
met friendly or not.

8. And lastly, be civil and courteous to foreigners, because the
danger of being uncivil and discourteous is so great, and is a danger
not only to you but to all your fellow-countrymen.

9. Always stand up for the honour of your own country, but
remember that others are equally bound to stand up for the honour
of theirs, and that the honour of your own country can never be
advanced by the people who live in it fighting for what is unjust and
wrong. Turn back to Chapter IX. and read the words at the beginning of it. In them you will find what Edmund Burke, one of the
wisest of our statesmen, thought about war and about the objects
for which alone it could rightly be begun.

10. These are his words: **"The blood of man should never be
shed but to redeem the blood of man. It is well shed for our
family, for our friends, for our God, for our country, for our
kind. The rest is vanity; the rest is crime."**

CHAPTER XIX.
EDUCATION.

"The fear of the Lord is the beginning of wisdom."
"Knowledge is power."

XXXVIII. WHAT EDUCATION MEANS.

1. IN the earlier chapters of this book you have been learning something about the laws and how they are made, something about the way in which our country is governed, something about the reasons why people have to pay rates and taxes. It is right and useful that every Australian boy and girl should be taught to understand something of the government of their own country; but perhaps some of you think that whether you know much or little about these other matters, at least you all know about **Education**—what it means, and what is the use of it.

2. When you hear people talking of education, it makes you think at once about going to school. Well, education means something more than **going to school**; but still, going to school is one great part of education, and it is just the part that we must think about now. If I were to begin by asking you why you come to school, I expect you would answer, quite rightly, that you come in order to learn.

3. And then, if I were to go on to ask you what it is you come to learn, you would most likely answer, reading, writing, and arithmetic. That is quite true, too, and yet there is something besides, which is quite as important—indeed, more important than even reading and writing.

Some Schoolroom Lessons.

4. In many schools there are wall-sheets on which are printed some of the great lessons that have to be taught and learnt in school. These are not lessons in geography, or arithmetic, or dictation, but in *habits of punctuality, of good manners and language, of cleanliness and neatness.* The pupils in the school are, in this way, as well as in other ways, made to feel the importance of *cheerful obedience to duty, of consideration and respect for others, and of honour and truthfulness in word and act.*

Precept and Practice.

5. It is quite certain that, if anyone thoroughly masters these lessons while he is at school, he will become, if he lives to grow up, a good and a useful citizen; but, if he has not learnt these lessons, then, though he may get a great deal of learning of a different kind, it will do him more harm than good. If a boy went on all through his school-life cheating at lessons whenever he had the opportunity, you would know that he had not learnt **"truthfulness in act,"** and you would have very little hope of his growing up an honourable, fair-dealing man.

6. And, again, if a boy takes advantage of his strength to tease and oppress those who are weaker than himself, you are sure that he has not learnt **"consideration and respect for others,"** and that he is likely to become one of those miserable people who care for nothing greater or higher than their own selfish pleasure.

7. So, once more, if a boy does his work sulkily and unwillingly, doing it only because he is obliged, and trying all he can to shirk it, then you know he has not learnt the lesson of **"cheerful obedience to duty,"** and you feel that such a boy will never be a useful citizen or do good service to his country, for he "shrinks when hard service must be done"; he even grudges taking enough trouble to do his common everyday work well.

8. So you will see for yourselves the truth of what I have said about the importance of these lessons beyond all other lessons. Over and over again, Britain has been faithfully and gloriously served by men who never had the chance of learning to read or write; but never in her whole history has she been truly served by men who had not learnt these other lessons of honour and truthfulness, of care for others, and of obedience to duty.

The King who could not Write.

9. You, most of you, know that, in old days, education was much less widely spread than it is now. You still find some old people, and a few middle-aged people too, who cannot read a book or sign their own names; if we could go back a hundred years, we should find the number of them still greater, and if we go back 800 years, we shall find a King of England in the same position—unable to sign his own name.

10. In the Cathedral library of **Canterbury** I have seen a piece of old yellow parchment with the name of **William the Conqueror** written upon it. After the name comes a mark, such as some uneducated people nowadays make when they are unable to write their own names. So, on this old parchment, some learned man had written the king's name for him, and the king had put his mark against it, to show that it was all right. Is it not strange to think that the William the Conqueror about whom you read in your histories did not know how to sign his own name?

XXXIX. SCHOOLS AND THEIR MANAGEMENT.

1. The people of Australia have, especially during the last thirty or forty years, bestowed a great amount of attention upon education, and have made very liberal provision for it. There are thousands of **primary schools**, hundreds of **colleges**, scores of **technical schools**, and four **universities** in the Commonwealth.

2. The Government of each State has said that, if eight or ten children can be got together regularly in any place, a teacher will be provided to instruct them. To help the Government in managing the schools in the different places, a certain number of men or women living in the neighbourhood of a school or several schools are elected to form what is called a *Board of Advice or School Board* for that school or schools.

3. The expense of building primary schools is paid out of the general revenue of the State—the public money—because they are meant for the public; and from the same source, also, the teachers' salaries are drawn.

Scholars.

4. The schools are there, but you will agree with me that if they are to stand empty, they might as well never have been built. Clearly, we must have scholars to fill them.

5. The best thing of all is when the children come of themselves, regularly and punctually; but, if the children are careless themselves about coming, and the parents do not take pains about sending them, then the truant or attendance officer has to find out why the child does not come to school. There may be some satisfactory reason, and then the child is excused; but if there is no good reason, the parent is first warned, and then, if he does not pay any attention to the warning, fined.

6. This compelling children to go to school is called "**compulsion**," or "**compulsory education**."

7. Sometimes it seems hard that children should be compelled to attend school when their parents would be very glad of their help at home; but then we have to remember that it is really better for everyone in the end that this should be so—better for the parents, better for the children, and better for the whole country—that the

MANUAL TRAINING CENTRE, PERTH.

children should be regularly taught while they are young than that they should have the great disadvantage of growing up in ignorance.

School Attendance.

8. It is a great mistake to think that, if you come to school irregularly, no one suffers but yourself. You suffer most, it is true, but the whole school suffers too. Not only does the credit of the school suffer, but if the attendance has been bad, the school may have to do with one teacher less than another school with the same number of children on the roll who attend regularly, and that must be a disadvantage.

9. It is very disappointing for the master to have to say, "I have a hundred scholars on the roll, but twenty of them have attended so badly that they have done the school more harm than good." You would think it very hard if you had to suffer for someone's wrongdoing, and yet, is it not just as hard if the school suffers because you, and others like you, have been negligent?

The Credit of the School.

10. Always remember that the well-doing of a school depends on the well-doing of every scholar in it. The Department of Education may build schools, the law may oblige children to attend, the teacher may give all his time and thought to teaching his classes, but neither Education Department, nor law, nor teacher can force a child to do his best if he does not care about it himself. And yet it is upon the children, as well as the teachers, setting themselves to do their very best, that the success and honour of the school depend.

11. It is true that the law has forbidden any child under fourteen years of age to go to work until he has obtained a Certificate of Exemption from Compulsory Attendance; but as soon as he has completed his fourteenth[30] year, he can leave school whether he has

30   This is so in New South Wales, Victoria, and Western Australia. In South Australia and Tasmania he may leave at thirteen; and in Queensland, at twelve.

obtained it or not. Some lazy scholars seem to think that when once they have obtained the certificate, they have done all that is required, and that it makes no difference whether they learn any more or not; but what a mistake they are making!

XL. Reading, Writing, and Something More.

1. Reading and writing are so common now, that just to be able to read and write and cipher will not enable anyone to get on in life. A boy must not only have learnt to read, he must have attended to what he has read and got good from it; he must not only know how to do a sum when it is set before him, but he must be able to apply his school arithmetic rules to the business of daily life, and know how to calculate measurements.

2. Some of you may have heard the story of Opie, the painter, when someone asked him what he mixed his colours with. "Brains, sir," answered the painter, meaning that, instead of going by any fixed rules out of a book, he thought for himself exactly what would be best for the piece of work he had in hand.

Eyes and no Eyes.

3. Take the case of two boys. They may know just the same amount to start with, they may be in the same class; but, if one of the two tries to make use out of school of the knowledge that he has gained, and to add more to it, he will soon leave far behind the other, who, as soon as the book is shut, thinks no more of what he has been reading.

4. Book learning is a great help, but it can never stand in the place of observation and thought.

5. Take, for example, a lesson in Physical Geography. All the boys may have learnt from the same book; they may all of them remember a good deal of what they have read, and be able to repeat it almost in the words of the book, but most likely they have never thought

SCHOOL OF MINES AND INDUSTRIES ADELAIDE.

of noticing for themselves any of the things which they have been reading about.

6. But suppose there is one boy who, when he is out walking, remembers what he has been reading, and compares it with what he sees round about him; such a boy will find, as soon as he begins to use his own eyes, that there are a whole number of questions that he wants to have answered, and that perhaps his book may help to answer for him; he will find that he has learnt enough in his walk to make the next geography lesson doubly interesting.

How to Rise.

7. In all the States the Government awards **scholarships**—that is to say, money prizes—to help a boy forward in his education. A boy who passes through all the classes in a primary school and does well may win one of these prizes, which will enable him to go on to a higher kind of school, where Latin, French, science, and many other subjects are taught. If he does well here, too, he may get another scholarship or exhibition (as it may be called), which will enable him, when he is old enough, to pass on to one of the Universities—Sydney, Melbourne, Adelaide, or Hobart; and in time he may become a doctor, a lawyer, an engineer, or a clergyman, and rise to the head of his profession.

Compulsion.

8. As I told you, education is now *compulsory*; that is to say, every parent is compelled to have his child educated. This was not always so. It was only in the year **1872** that Mr. J. Wilberforce Stephen brought in a Bill in the Victorian Parliament, which afterwards became the Education Act. By this Act, it was made part of the law that throughout the country schools should be established, and all the children within a reasonable walking distance of a school should be compelled to go to it, or be properly taught at home; and, since

ART GALLERY, HOBART

that time, it has become the law all over Australia that every child shall receive some education, and so be able to have a chance of rising and gaining a living when he or she grows up.

9. For you must understand that nowadays, when all the children in foreign countries are taught in good schools, it is quite necessary that Australian children should not be behindhand; otherwise all the work would certainly go to those who knew best how to do it, and the trade of our country would go to foreigners. It is not in Australia only that children are compelled to attend school; but they are equally obliged to do so in the United Kingdom, in America, in Germany, and in France.

Three Reasons for Going to School.

10. I have now given you the reasons why you should be glad to go to school, and to learn all you can while you are there.

11. In the first place, because the more you learn the more you will enjoy all the great books that have been written, the better you will understand the wonderful works of Nature, and the better use you will be able to make of its treasures.

12. In the second place, you should be glad to go to school, because by training your mind, and learning what history, geography, and science can teach, you will be better able to serve your country and be a good citizen.

13. And lastly, you should be glad to go to school, because it is only by the instruction you receive there that you can hope to get on in your trade or profession, whatever it may be, and to avoid being left behind by cleverer workers and quicker hands in foreign countries.

CHAPTER XX.
THRIFT.

"A penny saved is a penny gained."

XLI. EVERYONE OUGHT TO SAVE.

1. EVERYBODY in the country ought to try to save money against a rainy day, so that in old age, in time of sickness or distress, he may have something to fall back upon, and not be dependent upon others for support.

Why?

2. I need not spend much time in telling you why this is so, and why it is the duty of every man and woman, and, indeed, of every child, to put aside money in the Savings Bank, or in some other place where it will be kept safe and be ready for use in time of need. You have only to think a little for yourselves, and you will see the reason as plainly as I can tell you.

3. In the first place, it is a duty which every man owes to himself. Those who are young, and healthy, and strong find it sometimes hard to understand how terrible a thing it is to have bad times without any money saved.

4. Over and over again it happens that a good workman is unwise enough to depend upon his skill and his strength, and neglects to look forward. As long as there is work for him to do, or as long as his health and strength remain, he receives his wages and lives comfortably. But one day, work becomes slack, or he falls ill, or an accident

happens to him, and then, suddenly and without any warning, he finds himself face to face with poverty—unable to provide his food, unable to pay his rent, unable to pay his doctor.

Save Against Old Age.

5. Again, it may happen that a man has been fortunate enough to pass through the greater part of his life without any such misfortunes as those I have spoken of, and, at last, he finds old age coming on. Then, if he has saved nothing, he has to look forward to ending his days in sorrow and in misery, in a home without comfort or convenience, or, it may be, in the benevolent asylum itself.

6. In order that a man may not live in distress and die in poverty, it is his duty to save money.

Save To Help Others.

7. But there are few men and few women who have no one but themselves to think of. Husbands must provide for their wives, wives must help their husbands, parents must bring up and take care of their children. And so, if illness or accident overtakes any member of a family, there is generally sure to be some other member of the family who will have to bear the loss as well as the actual sufferer, and who will be unable to bear it without loss and trouble, unless a little money has been saved.

8. A man may be a good workman, and may never be idle or sick, yet if his wife or child is ill, he will have to spend money to relieve them just the same as he would have to do were he himself ill.

9. In order, therefore, that a man may support his family in time of trouble, it is his duty to save money.

Save To Keep Out Of The Benevolent Asylum.

10. And lastly, supposing a man or woman does not save, but when hard times come, or misfortune occurs, or old age is at hand, is unable to earn anything to support life, and is thus forced to go to the benevolent asylum or to accept an old-age pension from the Government, then we shall see directly that a real injustice is being done. For, of course, the benevolent asylum is not kept up for nothing, but is paid for by somebody; and that somebody is really the people who pay the taxes.

11. It very often happens that those who pay taxes have hard enough work to get their own living, and it is not fair that they who have managed to save and to avoid accepting an old-age pension should have to pay for the support of those who have been careless, and who, by their carelessness, have found themselves in utter poverty.

12. In order, therefore, that a man should not become a burden upon his neighbours, it is his duty to save money.

One More Reason For Saving.

13. These are three very good reasons why people should save and put by money for a rainy day, and there is one other reason which I must not leave out in a book which tells about our duties as "Good Citizens." Not only are saving and thrift most important and necessary for particular men and women, but it is of the greatest use to the country generally that all its citizens should be thrifty and saving.

14. It is only those who are free from want and poverty who can be contented, and it is only a country in which the greater number of the inhabitants are contented that can be really strong.

15. For all these reasons, therefore, it is a good thing to be thrifty and to save.

XLII. HOW TO SAVE.

1. But how are we to set about saving?—what is the best way to do it? There was a time when people used to think there was no better way of saving than putting their money into an old stocking and hiding it away. I dare say there are some old folks who do this still, but it is not a very wise plan to follow nowadays.

2. Supposing a man earns a shilling or a pound when he is thirty years old, and puts it away in a safe place till he is fifty. When he goes to look for it, he will find just exactly what he first saved, whether it is a shilling, or a pound, or twenty pounds, and no more. All the twenty years that the money has been laid up it will have been useless.

Savings Banks.

3. But supposing the same man, instead of locking his money up, puts it in the bank, then at the end of twenty years, instead of finding just what he first put in, he will find more than half as much again added to what he first earned. For the bank, instead of letting the money lie idle, will use it, lending it to people who are in want of it, spending it upon work which brings a profit, and so on; and they will pay the man who left the money with them so much a year for the use of it.

4. This payment is called "**interest**," and by adding the interest together, year after year, a man's savings will soon be doubled.

The Post Office Bank.

5. It is not necessary to have a great deal of money to be able to put it into a bank. All over Australia there are **Post Office Savings Banks** where anybody can put in any sum from a shilling upwards, and be sure of getting interest in return, till a certain amount is reached[31]. Every boy and girl, therefore, can begin to put money

31   The regulations as to the amount that can be deposited in a Savings Bank, and the interest that is paid, vary somewhat in the different States.

into the bank. All that is necessary is to go to the post office, get **a savings bank book**, and pay in the money which is to be saved.

Take Care Of The Pence.

6. In New Zealand there is even an easier way of saving little sums than this. A boy there can get at the post office little cards divided into twelve squares, which are on purpose to help children to save. Each square is meant to contain a penny stamp, which he can buy and stick on. When there are twelve stamps on the card, all he has to do is to take it to the post office again, and, in exchange for the twelve penny stamps, one shilling will be added to his savings, and put down in his bank book. So you see there is no reason why every penny should not be saved and put in the bank.

What Pennies Can Do.

7. It is wonderful how much can be done by saving little sums regularly. One of the most useful ways of saving is to put by money when one is young to buy what is called a **"pension"**—that is to say, a regular weekly payment to be received when one grows old, or becomes sick. For instance, if a young man at the age of nineteen puts by eightpence a week, or only a little more than a penny a day, he can be sure, when he reaches sixty years of age, to receive **a pension of 5s. a week**, and thus, whatever happens, he will never be quite without support in his old age.

8. Of course, it might happen that he died before reaching sixty years of age, and it would be hard in such a case if all the money he had put by were lost. Fortunately, it is not lost, for, in case of a man's death, whatever he may have paid is given to his relations.

9. In the same way, by saving little sums when you are young, you can insure your lives; that is to say, you can be sure that, on your death, a round sum of money will be paid to your family. In this way,

THE SAVINGS BANK, MARKET STREET, MELBOURNE

a man who has insured his life can be certain that, when he dies, his wife and children will not be left to starve.

10. It is a terrible thing for a man to feel that the comfort and welfare of those who are dearest to him depend upon his life only, and that, in case of his death, they have only misery and poverty to look forward to.

Clubs And Friendly Societies

11. Besides all the ways of saving money in which the Government helps, there are the ways which are provided by what are called **friendly societies** or **benefit clubs**.

12. Those who join these clubs agree to pay so much a year to the club, and, in return, they are sure of receiving help when they fall sick, or become too old to work. Each society or club has a different name, and some of them, such as the **Australian Natives**, the **Rechabites**, the **Foresters**, the **Druids**, and the **Oddfellows**, have a very large number of members and a great many subscriptions. They are very good institutions, not only because they are the means of helping those who are sick or unable to work, but because they encourage people to be thrifty and to save.

When To Begin Saving

13. It is never too early to begin to save. Remember this while you are young, and, if you are wise, you will begin at once to put by money in the bank; for a penny saved is not only a penny gained—it becomes, before long, a penny-halfpenny gained, and, if you wait long enough, twopence gained. Money that is wisely laid up is never idle; not only is it increasing from day to day and year to year, but, every day, it is helping to relieve the mind of the person who has saved it from anxiety and from the fear of being left in want and distress.

CHAPTER XXI
FREEDOM

"It is the land that freemen till,
That sober-minded Freedom chose,
The land, where girt with friends or foes,
A man may speak the thing he will."

— Tennyson

XLIII. AUSTRALIA IS A FREE COUNTRY

1. I dare say you have often heard people talk about Australia being a *Free Country*, and about the *Liberty* which we who live in Australia enjoy.

2. Fortunately for us, we live at a time when the very idea of being anything but free seems quite strange, and when some explanation is wanted of what is really meant by being without **freedom** and **liberty**.

3. But this was not always so. In times past, our ancestors in the old land were in many ways deprived of their freedom, and they enjoyed very little of the liberty which we now possess.

What Freedom Is

4. But before I go any further, and tell you how we, at the present day, have come to possess the freedom which our forefathers were without, I must try to explain to you what is meant by freedom, and why it is that we who enjoy it have so much to be thankful for.

5. Of course, when we use the word **freedom**, it is natural to think of somebody who has been actually imprisoned escaping

in some way from the place in which he is shut up. And there was indeed a time in Britain when innocent men and women were not sure even of freedom from imprisonment without trial. I shall tell you something about that later on. But, meanwhile, I want you to remember that there are other kinds of freedom which are even more important than that of merely going where one pleases.

6. Everyone in this country is now free to **think what he likes, to follow what religion he likes, to worship God in the way he chooses**, and, moreover, he is free **to try to persuade others of the truth of what he himself believes**. Besides this, as you know, we have in this country what is called *the* **liberty of the press**, which means that a man may write and print what he wishes without interference.

7. Then again, we have freedom in *buying* and *selling*; we may buy what we like and sell what we like. As I told you in another chapter, we have *freedom of election:* we may vote, without being interfered with, for the man whom we prefer to be a member of Parliament. Indeed, to put the whole matter quite shortly, we are free to do anything which is **not contrary to law and which does not tend to injure our neighbours.**

What We Are Not Free to Do

8. That is the only freedom which Britons are not allowed, and a moment's thought will show you that, if we were once allowed to do things which injured our neighbours, we should soon be in danger of losing our freedom ourselves. For instance, any of you, when you grow up and have votes, will be free, as I told you, to vote for any man you choose to be a member of Parliament; but you will not be free to try to compel other people to do so, for then you would at once be interfering with their freedom.

Trade Societies

9. And so, again, it is often very useful that those who are employed in the same kind of work—in weaving, in mining, in building, in machine-making, or in any other trade—should join together and make rules among themselves for their own advantage. When those engaged in one trade join together in this way, they form what is called a **Trades Union** or **Trade Society**, and they are able to do much good, and the members are able to help one another in many ways.

10. Sometimes those who belong to a Trades Union make it a rule that none of them will take less than a certain wage for their work, and they all agree that, unless they get as much as they think just and fair, they will not undertake the work at all. This is often a great help to the workers, and is sometimes the means of enabling them to get better wages and fairer treatment than they would if each man were to act for himself.

11. Sometimes, however, men belonging to societies of this kind have forgotten the true meaning of the word *freedom*, and have tried to *force* others to obey their rules, even though they have never consented to do so, and do not wish to be bound by them. Directly they do this, they are no longer the **friends of freedom**, but the **friends of tyranny**; for, though every man has the right to arrange what he will do about his own work, he has no right whatever to compel others to do the same.

12. It was when the Trades Unions were first started in England that these mistakes were sometimes made, and great harm was done in some places by those who used violence against their fellow-workmen. But nowadays, fortunately, the true meaning of **freedom of labour** is better understood than it used to be, and all the great Trades Unions now condemn any interference with the freedom of others.

XLIV. UNPLEASANT TRADES

1. Let me give you another instance of what I meant when I said that we were free to do anything which did not interfere with the freedom of others, or break the law.

2. There are a great many trades, such as the boiling of bones to make gelatine, the manufacture of vitriol, the tanning of hides for leather, and so on, which are very useful and very necessary, but which happen, for some reason or another, to be very unpleasant or very unwholesome; sometimes, as in the case of tanning and bone-boiling, because of the smells which arise during the work; sometimes, as in the case of the making of vitriol, because of the poisonous fumes which escape.

3. Now, everybody is free to become a bone-boiler, or a tanner, or a manufacturer of vitriol, and as long as he carries on any of these trades without injuring or interfering with others, none will object. But it may sometimes happen that, by opening his works in a particular neighbourhood, he may do great damage to those who live around; and, in that case, the law will step in and say that either he must do the work elsewhere, or that he must do it in such a way that those who live near shall not be injured. For though we are free to carry on what trade **we like, we are not free to carry it on to the injury of others.**

Sale of Dangerous Things

4. Again, you remember I told you that, in this country, everyone was free to buy and sell what he chose. But here again the same rule comes in. We are free to buy what we like and sell what we like, as long as we do no injury to others. But supposing a man sells gunpowder or poison, he is very likely to do great harm to his neighbours; for unless care be taken about the sale of such dangerous things, the gunpowder and the poison may easily fall into the hands of people who do not know their use, or who wish to use them for a bad purpose.

5. And so the law says that, though the sale of cloth, and sugar, and boots, and hats, and so on, is free, yet the sale of gunpowder and poison is not to be free, and that only those persons shall be permitted to sell these things who have been specially allowed to do so.

Liberty of the Press

6. In the same way, there are exceptions to the rule in other matters. I told you that we had, in this country, liberty of the press—that is to say, that everyone was free to write and to print what he chose. Nevertheless, there are some things which, although we enjoy this liberty, we are not allowed to write or to print. The same rule applies here as in the case of the sale of gunpowder and the manufacture of vitriol. We are free to do what we like as long as, by so doing, we do not harm other people. But directly we begin to use our liberty to injure or annoy others, then the law will interfere and prevent us.

7. For instance, if a man were to write and print in a book or newspaper an accusation against one of his neighbours, saying that he was dishonest or untrustworthy in his trade, or had been guilty of some crime against the law, then his neighbour would have the right to go to law against him, and to have the writer punished either by being sent to prison or by being fined a sum of money.

The Abuse of Liberty

8. A rule of this kind is indeed most useful, for, in these days, when newspapers and printing and cheap postage have made it so easy for people to spread abroad reports about others, a terrible power is put into the hands of those who choose to use it for a bad purpose. It often happens that more harm is done to a man or a woman by spreading a false report, or telling an unkind story about them, than could be inflicted upon them by any mere violence or actual bodily injury.

9. For instance, suppose anybody were to write a letter to the

BOTANICAL GARDENS SHOWING RIVES REACH, BRISBANE.

papers to say that a tradesman used false weights, or gave his customers sugar with sand in it, or tea which was half sweepings, there can be no doubt whatever that the poor grocer or tea-dealer, or whoever it might be, would suffer very much, and lose a great deal of custom. It would be no excuse for the person who made the charge to say afterwards that he found it was not true, for the harm would have been done, and the right and fair answer to make to him would be, "You should have taken the trouble to find out the truth before you accused your neighbour; you chose to judge him hastily, and you must take the consequences."

The Power of Newspapers

10. Unhappily, what is written in the newspapers nowadays is read by so many people, and in so many different places, that, when a false or unjust statement is once made, it is often quite impossible to undo the harm which it has occasioned; for many people read the charge who never see the reply to it. This ought to make people very careful indeed how they speak, and still more how they write harsh and cruel things about others. It is well indeed that the law, while it allows perfect liberty of the press to all who know how to use that liberty wisely, makes an exception in the case of those who use their liberty to injure others.

The Rule of Liberty

11. These examples which I have been giving you are all intended to teach you what is the true meaning of **freedom** and **liberty**, and what is the right use to be made of it. You and I enjoy far greater liberty than our forefathers did, and very thankful we ought to be that we have no longer to suffer as they had for the right to think, to write, to speak, to act as we please. But, at the same time, we must remember that, if more has been given to us, more will be expected of us.

12. We must never forget that we live in a world in which there are many millions of people besides ourselves, and that it is our bounden duty to live our own lives and to do our own work in such a way as not to interfere with or cause pain to others. The simple rule, "**Do unto others as you would they should do unto you**," is a very good one to bear in mind whenever we talk of our right to do this, that, and the other. We ought always to think of our duties together with our rights; and what our duties are, the rule you have just read will always tell you plainly enough.

13. You know that **very young children** and **mad people** are not allowed their freedom, for fear they should do some harm to themselves or to others. It is only those who are supposed to have knowledge and experience to whom perfect liberty is allowed. By using our freedom wrongly, we may show that, like young children and madmen, we are unfit to be trusted with it. It is by using it rightly, for the good of others as well as for our own good, that we can best show that we are wise enough and strong enough to possess so great a treasure as freedom really is.

CHAPTER XXII
HOW OUR FREEDOM WAS WON

"For freedom's battle once begun,
Bequeathed by bleeding sire to son,
Though baffled oft, is ever won."

— *Byron*

XLV. OUR FREEDOM IS NEW

1. NOW I have told you something about the meaning of the word *freedom*, and how far we in this country are free to do and say what we like without interference. But, as I said before, you must not suppose that the freedom which we now enjoy was always possessed by English-speaking men and women.

2. On the contrary, it is because our present liberty has been won for us by our forefathers only by great sacrifices, and has been bought with their fortunes and their lives, that we value it so greatly, and are so proud of possessing it. I spoke to you of freedom of thought, and said that a man was free in our country, at the present day, to think what he chose; but you who have read your British history know only too well that this was not always so.

Freedom of Thought.

3. It was one of the best and purest of Englishmen, **Sir Thomas More**, who, in the reign of Henry VIII, was sent to prison, tried, condemned, and at last beheaded because he would not say that he believed the king was the true head of the Church to which he belonged. The king and those who advised him declared that everyone

should take what was called the **"Oath of Supremacy"**; but More replied that, though he was quite ready to serve the king truly and well, yet his conscience would not allow him to take the oath in the way the king commanded.

4. But, in those days, it was not enough that a man should act according to the law—it was necessary that he should also think that which those who made the law wished him to think. Sir Thomas More was willing enough to obey King Henry, but, in his own heart, he did not believe that the claim which Henry had made to be head of the Church was a right one.

5. This was an offence which could not be forgiven, and More was sent to the Tower; and, after suffering a long and painful imprisonment, was at last beheaded in the year 1535.

6. A very different man from Sir Thomas More was **Hugh Latimer**, Bishop of Worcester; but in one thing he resembled him—he, too, was put to death because he would not give up the right which all of us nowadays have, of believing what his conscience told him was right.

7. It was in the reign of Queen Mary that Latimer, with another famous bishop, **Thomas Ridley,** was burnt at Oxford on account of his religion. The words of Latimer as he stood at the stake have become famous: "Be of good comfort, Master Ridley," said he, "and play the man. We shall this day light such a candle, by God's grace, in England, as I trust shall never be put out."

8. Not only did these words prove true—not only did the cause for which Latimer gave up his life grow stronger and prosper through the example of his death—but the cause of freedom of thought in England, and throughout the world, was helped by the suffering which he and many others like him underwent for conscience' sake.

9. It was not More and Latimer alone who gave up their lives rather than deny what they believed to be true; nor was it only for their religious views that Englishmen were persecuted. There have been hundreds and thousands of brave men and women in our history—high

and low, rich and poor—who have stood up for freedom of thought just as truly as the Lord Chancellor and the bishop of whom I have spoken. It is to their courage that we owe our liberty at the present day.

Freedom of the Press.

10. But freedom of thought was not the only freedom which was denied to our forefathers and which is enjoyed by us.

11. You know, in the last chapter, I told you something about the **liberty of the press** which we now enjoy, and I explained to you that, as long as we do not injure others by what we write, we who live in this country are free to write and to print what we choose. But this freedom, of which we are so proud, was a thing unknown to our ancestors.

12. We, who are accustomed, as a matter of course, to read in a newspaper—which we can buy for a penny—news from every part of the world, may well be astonished to find that, only as far back as the reign of Charles II, the Lord Chief Justice of England, one of the highest judges in the land, declared that, by the law of England, it was criminal to publish *any public news*, whether true or false, without the king's leave.

13. And, indeed, when persons were unfortunate enough to offend against the laws by printing what was not permitted, or what was not approved of by those who had power and high position, the punishments which were inflicted upon them were often very severe, and often, too, very unjust.

XLVI. PRYNNE.

1. In the reign of Charles I, for instance, **William Prynne**, a lawyer, wrote a book which was displeasing to the king and his friends, and, for so doing, he was condemned to stand twice in the pillory, and to have his ears cut off. Nor was this cruel treatment thought to be punishment enough. Prynne was fined £5,000, was turned out

PRYNNE IN THE PILLORY.

of his college at the University of Oxford, and was prevented from doing his work as a lawyer.

2. But not even these penalties could shake his determination or compel him to be silent. He wrote another book, and, this time, it was the Archbishop of Canterbury whom he offended. Again, he was put in the pillory, his cheeks were branded with a hot iron, another fine was imposed upon him, and he was thrown into prison. Even then, however, he did not cease writing, and, at last, his courage met with its reward.

3. His sufferings had won people to his cause, and, in the year 1640, he was elected a member of Parliament; and though, during the rest of his life, he more than once got into further troubles by the boldness of his writing, he did much—both by his endurance and by his sufferings—to help on **the cause of the freedom of the press**, for which he had fought so long.

Cobbett.

4. Let me give you another example for which we need not go back so far. It was only in the year 1810, or just over a hundred years ago, that **William Cobbett**, who afterwards became a member of Parliament, was tried and punished for writing things which anybody nowadays could say and write without any interference whatever.

5. He believed that some militiamen had been unfairly punished, and, in a paper which belonged to him, he spoke of the injustice of the treatment which they had suffered, and blamed those who ordered the punishment. He was brought before the judges, was tried, found guilty, and sentenced to be sent to prison for two years and to pay a fine of £1,000.

6. So you will see that the **freedom of the press** which we enjoy was, like **freedom of thought**, only won by the sufferings of those who lived before our time.

Other Instances.

7. I might give you many more instances of the way in which the freedom we enjoy, as a matter of course at the present day, has only been won for us bit by bit, by the courage, the suffering, and the determination of those who lived before us.

8. Some of you have, perhaps, been at a great public meeting, and have heard a well-known speaker make a speech to thousands of listeners—about Parliament, about an election, or about all sorts of other matters which interest people. No one interferes with such a speaker nowadays, for we have **freedom of public meeting**. But this was not always so in Britain; and, over and over again, meetings have been broken up by armed men, and both the speakers and the listeners have been imprisoned and punished for daring to take part in such a thing.

9. And so, again, the **freedom to travel** where we like and when we like is a new thing. The **freedom to buy what we like and to sell what we like**, and to get the best price we can for what we sell, is a new thing; and there are many other examples. But I think I have said enough to show you how precious a thing is the freedom which we really have, and how terrible it would be to go back to the old state of things where men were punished and persecuted for doing the very things which you and I and all of us do every day, and which we think the commonest and most harmless things in the world.

What We Owe to Our Forefathers.

10. It is for these reasons that we need never tire of reading and studying the history of those to whom we owe so much. In the first place, their example is full of encouragement and help to us, for there are many things which we may have to do as citizens of this great new country which we shall do better if we imitate the courage and the endurance of those who did so much to make the old country—our Mother-land—truly great.

11. And, in the second place, we must not forget that the battle which they fought is not really won yet, but that the cause of freedom has still to be struggled for in many parts of the world; and, indeed, the freedom which we have is not, after all, so sure and so complete that we may not ourselves have some day to give up our best possessions and our lives to keep what we have won even in this country.

CHAPTER XXIII.
WATCHWORDS OF ENGLISH LIBERTY.

"To none will we sell, to none will we deny, to none will we delay, right and justice."

— *Magna Carta.*

XLVII. CHARTERS AND STATUTES.

1. THE freedom which we now have has, as I told you in the last two chapters, been won by the struggles and suffering of a great number of men at different times in our history and in different ways. Sometimes it has been gained by hard fighting on the battlefield; at others, by eloquent speeches and hard, patient work in Parliament. Some, again, have been won only after those who did most to obtain them had suffered martyrdom and lost their lives at the stake or on the scaffold.

2. But there is hardly one of our great liberties which has not, at one time or another, been made part of the law of the country, and written down in plain terms, so that no one afterwards would have any doubt as to what was the real law of the land.

3. It is in the great **Charters** and in the great **Statutes** of the country that these famous laws have usually been written down. The **Charters** are the records of the rights which the kings of England have, from time to time, granted to the people. The **Statutes** are the **Acts of Parliament** which have been passed by the Lords and Commons, and approved of by the King.

4. I am going, in this chapter, to say something about a few of these written rules upon which so much of our liberty depends. That you may see why I do so, let me remind you of two important facts. First,

the **King** is the head of our judicature, or system of dispensing justice; and, secondly, in its foundation principles and main provisions, the **laws** that have been made and are being made by the Commonwealth Parliament and by the Parliaments of the States **are founded on the law of England**. That we in Australia can make laws for ourselves at all is because the Mother-country has allowed us to do so. It was in **1828** that the British Parliament sanctioned the establishment of a **legislature in New South Wales**, with power to make laws for the people within its borders; and the **Commonwealth Parliament** acquired its **power to make laws for all Australia** by virtue of a provision in the Act to constitute the Commonwealth of Australia, which, as you remember, was passed by the Imperial Parliament in **1900**.

5. As our freedom of action is so dependent on the state of that possessed by the people of the United Kingdom, and on what they deem to be fair and right, we should seek to know as much as we can concerning their struggle to obtain the liberty they now enjoy.

6. The most ancient and the most famous of the written charters upon which our present liberties are founded is

Magna Carta.

7. Here is a passage from it:—

"No free man shall be taken, or imprisoned, or dispossessed,[32] **or outlawed, or exiled, or injured in any other way, except by the lawful judgment of his peers,**[33] **or by the law of the land."**

8. The meaning of that is plain enough. It means that everybody shall always be entitled to a free and a fair trial, according to law. If, indeed, this great rule had never been disobeyed, many an unjust and cruel judgment which has been given at one time or another in the history of the English people would have been avoided. But though our ancestors sometimes fell short of their own laws, still it

32   Turned out of his property.
33   Equals.

KING JOHN SEALING "MAGNA CARTA."

was always a great thing to have the rule before them to point out what was true justice and wisdom.

Old Laws, Good and Bad.

9. Sometimes you will hear people talk as if laws were bad or useless only because they are old and were made a very long time ago. This is true enough of some laws—those, for instance, which have to do with manners and customs which frequently change. But it is not true of laws which have to do with the great rules of right and wrong, which are as true now as they were 800 years ago, and will be equally true 800 years hence.

10. It is very foolish, therefore, to say that any law is a bad one merely because it is an old one.

11. It is necessary to ask first what the law is before we can say whether it is bad or good. For instance, where do we find this great rule which I told you about just now—this rule which says that "**no man shall be judged except by his equals and according to the law of the land**"? The lawyers would tell you that it is to be found in chapter 9 Henry III.; that is to say, in the **ninth chapter of the Statutes passed in the reign of Henry III.; and Henry III.**, as you know, came to the throne in 1216, or nearly 700 years ago.

12. But the way the lawyers put it is not the way we who are not lawyers generally describe it. We say that it is **rule thirty-nine of the Great Charter**, commonly called "**Magna Carta**," granted by King John to the Barons of England at Runnymede, on behalf of the people of England, in the year 1215. And certainly we should be making a great mistake if we called this a bad law just because it is nearly 700 years old.

Another Gift of the Charter.

13. Then there is another great rule in this same Magna Carta which puts into words the true secret of justice, and shows that, so long ago as the time of King John, Englishmen knew that, in order that the law

might be of any real use, it should be open to all alike—rich and poor, high and low—and that it should not only be open to everyone to claim his rights through the law, but that everyone should be able to have his claim listened to and attended to immediately, and not be put off from day to day and month to month without justice being done him.

14. In rule forty of the Great Charter you will find these words:—

"To none will we sell, to none will we deny, to none will we delay, right and justice."

Promise and Performance.

15. This is a splendid promise made by the King to the people. If the promise had always been kept by those whose business it was to see justice done, much wrong and much suffering would have been avoided.

16. Unfortunately, there have been many times in British history when judges and magistrates have been found wicked enough to **sell their judgments** to those who were rich enough to buy them, and have refused them to those who were too poor to do so.

17. There have been times when those who sought justice have been **denied it**, and because they were weak, or friendless, or disliked, have asked in vain for the rights the law gave them. And lastly, there have been times when those who sought for justice have been put off, and the hearing of their cause has been **delayed**, until, when right was at last done to them, it came too late to be of any benefit. So you will see that, despite King John's promise to the Barons, right and justice have been sold, denied, and delayed.

18. But though there have been, and perhaps still may be, cases in which the rule has been broken, yet, on the whole, it has been a good thing to have it clearly written down for everybody to see and for everybody to appeal to. And the very fact of having such a rule as part of the law of the land has been an advantage, although, at times, the rule may not have been observed. For though there have been some bad judges and unjust magistrates in our history, yet, on the whole, there

is no country in the world where the judges have, as a rule, been more upright and honourable, and where justice has been done more regularly and with greater certainty, than in Britain and its dependencies.

XLVIII. HABEAS CORPUS.

1. Some of you may perhaps have heard people talk about what is called a "**Habeas Corpus**." The name is certainly not one which tells us much; it is made up of two Latin words which mean "*Take the body*." But though the name is a puzzling one, it has very often been used in our history, for it has to do with one of the great rules of which we have been speaking, by which our freedom is made certain. There was a time, as I have told you, when men and women in England might be taken to prison without just cause, and kept there for months, and sometimes for years, without having a fair trial, or indeed any trial.

2. Of course, it was very little use for the law to say, as it did in Magna Charta, that every man had a right to be tried by his equals. If he were never brought to trial, the rule plainly did not help him at all.

3. Much injustice was done, and much suffering was inflicted, by the bad and shameful plan of imprisoning men without trial, and many were the complaints that were made against it. It was not, however, till the year 1679, in the reign of King Charles II., that an Act of Parliament was passed which gave a right to every person in the kingdom to claim a fair trial within a reasonable time, and which did more than that, for it not only gave the right, but what was of still greater importance, it gave a means by which the poorest and most unprotected could insist upon the right being really granted to him.

4. This famous Act of Parliament, which is usually called the **Habeas Corpus Act**, declares that, if any man or woman be imprisoned, whether by the King or by the order of any court of justice, he or she, or their friends on their behalf, may have what is called a "**writ of Habeas Corpus**," which is really an order to the governor of the gaol where the person is imprisoned, or to anyone else who keeps him imprisoned,

to bring him before a judge who may determine whether or not his imprisonment is just.

5. Of course, if the law went no farther than this, it would be of very little use, for there would be no way of making bad judges or magistrates give the order required. But there is something more, for the law further says that every judge or magistrate, or other person who has the right to give a **writ of Habeas Corpus**, must do so, and that, if he refuses, he shall at once be liable to pay a fine.

6. So that it is not likely that anyone nowadays would be long without the order he wanted.

7. The reason why the words "Habeas Corpus" are used is because they are the first words in the order, which used to be written in Latin. The words, as I told you, mean "*Take the body*;" and the order, or writ, commanded the person to whom it was sent to bring up the "**body**" or **person** of the prisoner for trial, so that he might be found guilty or innocent, and punished or released accordingly.

The End of Slavery.

8. In Chapter XIV. I told you that no man could be a slave on British soil. In the year 1772 a negro slave named **Somerset** was turned out into the street by his cruel master, because he was ill and unable to work. The slave was found almost dead in the streets by **Mr. Granville Sharp**, who, being a kind and humane man, had him taken to the hospital, and found a situation for him when he got well.

9. Two years afterwards, Somerset's old master met him, and at once told a policeman to put him into prison as a runaway slave. "He is my property," said the master, "and no one has any more right to take him away than to take my hat or my coat." Mr. Sharp and the master went to law to settle the dispute, and the Lord Mayor of London, who had to try the case, at once declared that Somerset was free, and that his old master had no right to claim him. The master tried to carry off Somerset again; and, at last, the whole matter came before the judges. It was

then that **Lord Mansfield**, speaking on behalf of twelve of the judges, declared that, by the law of England, a man becomes free the moment he touched British soil.

10. This great judgment has become another watchword of our freedom, and, from the time when it was spoken, there could never any longer be a doubt that slavery in the United Kingdom or any British dependency was at an end for ever.

The Use of Watchwords.

11. What I want you to understand in all these examples is that, besides gaining a new liberty or a new right, it is always a good thing, both for ourselves and for those who come after us, that it should be written down clearly in the shape of a law, a charter, the sentence of a judge, or in some other solemn form, so that not only may there be no uncertainty about it in the future, but that all men may be able, ever afterwards, to refer to the very words themselves and to say—That IS THE LAW.

The great lesson of this book will be found very shortly on the slate below.

THE NUMBERS ON THE SLATE WERE SHOWN BY FLAGS
HOISTED ON THE MAST; BY THIS MEANS THE MESSAGE
WAS CONVEYED TO ALL THE SHIPS IN THE FLEET.